About the Author

Angela Gabriela Horne holds a BSc in Chemistry from University of London. She has had many careers including a brief stint as a bridal wear fashion model, a roulette dealer at an elite London casino, and an investment banker—a dealer on a trading floor. But, she always dreamed of writing a book that would change the way people think and transform their lives.

Angela lives in south London with her father, her sister, brother-in-law and a rather large cat. *Meditations of a Former Statue* is her first book. She is working on her next book: a transcendental love story revealing the hero in every man.

For occasional free chapters and stories, visit her at https://angelagabrielahorne.com.

For
Giustina Caprio Dutta
1934–2020
Romanina Rea Contucci
1927–2020
Chinmoy Datta
1934–2020
Mahesh Dhokia
1953–2020
Gary Jacob Horne
1962–2020

Contents

1. San Francisco – Dreams in Stone 1
2. Meeting 7
3. Eleanor 13
4. Xoran/James 19
5. Xavier/David 25
6. Eleanor and James 29
7. The Swords: Clarity and Brilliance 35
8. The Day I Refuse to Remember – 25,000 Years Ago 39
9. Who am I? 45
10. The Way of Lies 49
11. My Days 53
12. Grace Cathedral Part I 57
13. Grace Cathedral Part II 63

14.	The Way of Shame	69
15.	Honour, a Meditation	75
16.	Dreams	79
17.	The Impotence of Reason	83
18.	Code of Courage	91
19.	The Download	95
20.	The Planet	99
21.	Memoir	103
22.	No Turning Back	107
23.	Only a Statue Knows	111
24.	Thunder	113
25.	Music	121
26.	God Knows	127
27.	Waiting	129
28.	Mercy	133
29.	A Meditation on Romance	135
30.	Divine Love	145
31.	Peace	149
32.	A Little Piece of Hell	153
33.	The Power of Witness	173
34.	I Don't Know	177
35.	Anger	183

36.	Warrior of Thought	189
37.	Awakening	195
38.	Pressure	197
39.	The Dance of Creativity	201
40.	A Strange Energy	207
41.	My Dark Nights	211
42.	Transcendence	223
43.	Questions	229
44.	Darkness	233
45.	Radiance	237
46.	Entertain The Thought	241
47.	September	245
48.	Peace II	249
49.	The Wise Ruler Returns	251
50.	A Comet	253
51.	Interstellar	255
52.	Speak to Me	259
53.	Tension	263
54.	The Promise	265
55.	Writing Down the Story	267
56.	Clara is Real	275
57.	Sadness	277

58.	Integrating	279
59.	Acceptance	281
60.	The Lonely Hours	285
61.	Play	287
62.	Desire	289
63.	Tell The Truth	295
64.	A Comet	297
65.	Golden Gate Park	301
66.	Hello	307
67.	Eleanor and David	309
68.	The First Blessing	315
Acknowledgements		319

1

SAN FRANCISCO – DREAMS IN STONE

I don't remember when I became stone. Hiding in a mountain cave for twenty-five thousand years plays havoc with my memory. It is strange to start in the middle of the story. Please be patient with me: the hours and the centuries have been lonely.

From that cave in the mountains of southern Italy near Monte Cassino, I was sculpted into a statue by a penniless English artist, living in Italy, whose love had been spurned by an heiress. Marcus hid for many weeks in that cave to heal his broken heart. Within months he had sculpted my present form as a statue out of a boulder of fine marble hewn from the cave wall.

In 1915, he sold this, his greatest work, to an English nobleman who then donated me to the Royal Botanic Gardens at Kew in England. I remained there for one hundred years, nestled inside the wisteria temple. The fronds of the hardy Chinese plant twirled around the iron-domed framework built in 1820. With the passing century and the cool English climate, the fronds became elaborate branches twisting, turning, becoming sturdy enough to, in turn, support the iron frame now fragile with rust.

Today, I am in the sacred City of San Francisco as a recent gift from the Mayor of London to commemorate an international partnership for peace and prosperity between these two great cities. I am in Golden Gate Park. The peace here heals my soul.

Statues feel no cold, no heat, no pain nor joy. There has been safety in stone. I observe but do not feel. Too many emotions, like a severe frost, and my stone form would crack and crumble. I would be vulnerable.

I always believed there was safety in stone; if I could feel nothing then nothing could hurt me. However, I can speak into the hearts of those whose hearts are open. A voice from the heart is the most powerful voice of all.

My prayers will soon be answered. I had longed to meet a poet. I have waited centuries for her. I am tormented each day by the horrors I have witnessed during my time in stone. The horror of war has exceeded even the crimes I committed against humanity when I was a trusted ruler in my former life.

I thought I could atone for my past crimes by imprisoning my spirit in stone for fifty thousand years: one year for every human life lost in battle that day – my last day as a human being. The day I refuse to remember. But the cries, the screams come back at night to haunt me. Burying memories in stone does not dissolve them. They are a heavy weight on my soul.

My enemy has returned. Through his treachery, I lost my empire. Through my fear and foolishness, I did not see past his trickery and I precipitated that unjust war. Today, he has become human again and holds high office within the United States government's Department of Defense. His office has no public accountability. He has the freedom to operate within the shadows of great power. I fear greatly for humanity. He is about to unleash wars of such magnitude that will forever destroy the human spirit. The signs are already here. They are the same before any war: a culture of fear and lies, of innocent ideas twisted for personal gain, of nationalistic fervour and mistrust, of peoples misled. But I can do nothing. I am stone.

I must heal. I must transform. I yearn for absolution for the many crimes I committed in my past. Did I cause the present world of fear and scarcity? That battle, that day I refuse to remember, was the turning point in human history. I must heal, but only a poet can set me free.

My name is Clara.

Please sit with me and hear my story. I promise you wisdom. I promise peace.

Allow me to introduce my friends and protectors: Polaris and Aurora, majestic golden eagles, swift, and sure like my horses.

How I miss my horses. But they are another story.

Polaris circles at over five thousand feet above me and patrols the San Francisco Bay Area. Aurora flies at a lower altitude. She hunts and guides while Polaris watches over us all.

One afternoon, Polaris hovered in his usual patrol flight. He soared in celebration. His cry floated as silk through the sunshine across the bay. A large aircraft was approaching San Francisco International airport. This aircraft had flown over five thousand miles from London. The poet was on that aircraft. She was here at last. She had heard my call, my entreaties to her heart. She did not know who I was, but she came.

Her name was Eleanor.

To follow the heart's call takes courage. In a world led by reason and logic, to follow the heart may be considered foolish and dangerous. But it is far more dangerous to ignore the heart and focus only on the rational mind. It takes spiritual maturity to listen and follow intuition. I have one warning: an open heart is useless without strength to stand firm in the face of confusion and lies. The lies, unknowingly believed, weaken and imprison the misled. The lies, uncovered and cleared, release and strengthen the seeker.

I was always armed with two swords. One, named Brilliance, was bequeathed to me by my father. It had a diamond the size of a large walnut set in the pommel. The other, named Clarity, was bequeathed by my mother. Clarity had a rare blue-violet diamond of similar size set in its pommel. These were not mere ceremonial swords. They had drawn blood. They were entrusted to me to clear away doubt, shadows, and confusion: these grey qualities were always the harbingers of evil. I was an empress. My sacred duty was to protect and ensure my people flourished in prosperity and peace. That was an ancient time. My empire no longer exists. All records were lost in the destruction of the Library of Alexandria four hundred years after the birth of the one known as The Christ.

One of my many regrets.

My shameful history may be lost but a wealth of human knowledge and learning has also disappeared. Who knows, if the library had survived, would Alexandria be as prominent as London or New York today?

Hell is full of regrets, dark and grey. Classic colours of hell are always shades of dull grey without hope of silver: grey with a dash of dried blood here and there. Even the December clouds over London are a dried-blood red at night. I missed the stars on those nights. In San Francisco, however, I am grateful for the summer fog from the Pacific Ocean that comes each day and blesses the city. The fog is a kiss from a faithful lover that fades by noon only to return with fresh passion the next morning.

The hell I live each day is of my own making. On that day I refuse to remember, I had invoked the Angel of Compassionate Condemnation. He helped me create my present imprisonment in stone. I spend many nights in deep contemplation here in Golden Gate Park. From sunset until dawn the names of the dead are whispered to me one by one through the redwoods as stories in the wind. Only I can hear the names, the many stories. This is my private sacred hell because I can do nothing. I have no power as a statue until my heart is awakened. I must learn to feel again, both joy and suffering.

I am afraid.

Only Eleanor can help me. She has the courage to follow her heart to an unknown land far from her home, far from the woman she once knew herself to be.

2

MEETING

Eleanor came to see me. Aurora flew low over the park and enticed her to come to me. It is hard to ignore a magnificent eagle flying over your shoulder. To feel the turbulence of an eagle's wing against your face is an awakening in itself.

'You are so fragile,' I said into her heart.

'There is strength in vulnerability,' Eleanor said. Her face was serene with a delicate lace of sorrow – her eyes empty; she had no more tears.

What did she mean by her words? I did not understand. I could see her heart was broken and that she was in great pain. But there was a firm resolve in her demeanour. She was following guidance from her heart even though she did not know why. Her courage moved me. She, too, had been damaged by lies. Her lover had lied to her. He had grown bored of her simple innocence and craved the apparent excitement of women who were independent, rich and successful. The lies Eleanor believed created self-doubt – that most dangerous enemy of the human spirit. But she was strong. Anyone else would have accepted defeat. She fought on through the lies and confusion. She came to this foreign land far from her home and would soon discover her true self untarnished by allegiance to false gods.

'Never, ever surrender your dreams,' I said.

'I don't know what they are anymore.' Eleanor said.

'Stand firm with a soft and open heart and they will become clear.'

The fog of the unknown is the path of any creative venture. How can you create if you already know how it will end?

I digress.

Eleanor smiled and walked away to her new life.

Perhaps it may have seemed strange to visit a statue in Golden Gate Park and hear a voice and words that made little sense. Life is certainly stranger than fiction. I missed her, but I was happy. She was in California at last. I knew she would come back to see me.

November 2nd is the day of the dead. On that day the voices from the trees are loudest. I hear the names of the dead, one by one as a prayer for their souls. The Angel of Compassionate Condemnation appeared again.

'Those are the names of the dead who pray for you, Clara,' he said, his tone so soft and low that the branches of the trees resonated, leaves falling around us in time with the dancing feathers of his enormous luminous wings. 'Self-doubt is the most dangerous of all poisons to the human spirit.'

This was no ordinary angel. He was big, at least forty feet tall from his feet to the carpal joint of his wings. He was my companion in this hell of my own making.

'What have I done to merit your faith in me?'

'I am here to help you understand the power of the human heart,' he smiled. 'You were not always stone. Soon you will learn and you will remember.'

To be born again, to be free of this hell, I am to help Eleanor recover her faith in her path. I feel nothing, but this safety and remoteness will no longer serve my destiny. Eleanor's life is in danger. My enemy will find her and harm her unless I protect her from his evil. It is normal to eventually leave your body, but there is no fate worse than losing your soul. Everyone deserves a new beginning. When all hope is lost and faith destroyed, only then can a new light appear showing the way to a new world.

Is there music in the morning fog? Each city has its own rhythm. The bass tones of London and the jazzy tremolos of San Francisco; each city resonates with my heart. Each city has its own unique elegance. My disguise will soon crumble. No longer am I remembered. Who am I? I have ceased to be in the memory of others. Those who once knew my name, no longer exist. A civilisation that passed many millennia since.

How does my enemy find me? He uses Eleanor. He meets her at an East Coast benefit for a non-profit organisation and follows her here. He has her watched. She is unaware of the constant surveillance. Her life is violated. They saw her come and visit me. They saw the hilts of my swords in stone.

Why is it so hard to trust the voice in my heart? The rational mind is useful, but it is only a servant of the outside world. The most defining reality comes from within, always.

I do not know how to help her. But in my dream, the Angel comes to me and unlocks my heart. The names of the dead flow through me. I feel the pain in waves through my stone form and my heart breaks. It is reformed, stronger, lighter. My whole being crumbles. The fog cloaks me at dawn and the dream fades. The names of the dead are now silent.

Dreams never die, I just lose sight of them sometimes. There is not much to say today. When the glare of the city lights reflect off the blanket of fog in San Francisco turning the sky amber red, I feel so alone. Only lonely desolation reminds me of my once human form. She came to me in trust. I had waited so many centuries. But everything must come to pass.

I seem a lonely ambassador, meek in heralding a new world of courage. The world today, as we know, is of a fear deep and unquestioned. Eleanor will soon be ready. She does not know what is required of her but she has the strength and the courage for the task. What use is an open heart and an open mind without the strength and discipline to take actions that are uncomfortable in a world of fear? Those same actions may be normal in a world of love. To remove one's armour takes far more courage than to protect oneself with an impenetrable shield.

I speak with authority: it was my cowardice that eventually brought about today's world. I had succumbed to the fear and uncertainty of my ministers and foolishly agreed to a bloody campaign to quell a border dispute with my enemy King Xoran of the Land of Shadows. This campaign proved to be a costly distraction. My casualties mounted daily. I received word of another army marching from the south. The Realm of Light were attacking us? This could not be. I was blind to the realities on the ground and trusted my ministers who had been corrupted by spies from my enemy. I ordered a counter-offensive with a depleted force.

Since that day I refuse to remember, I have been as a ruler in disguise. I have watched and learned for myself. The lessons culminated in the twentieth century, since the birth of the one known as Jesus Christ, were the bloodiest in human history. Fifty-six million people died in the war known as World War Two. I have seen endless military cemeteries nestled on that Italian mountainside between spruce and cedar trees. I have seen the rosaries rusting on the white marble-cross grave stones. Young men who had fallen at nineteen or twenty years old. What myth such heroic sacrifice: an insult to the creator of these fine young human beings. I brought about a world where such slaughter is routine. Ancient military history is always relevant to the modern world. The stories have not changed. Lies and fear always precede war.

We are in the most dangerous time of all. The earth is in transition to a new world. It is a shift that takes place every twenty-five thousand years. A battle is raging between belief systems that advocate scarcity and those that know that everyone can prosper. A similar awakening occurred in the decade nineteen hundred and sixty years since the birth of The Christ. My enemy, in a former lifetime, engineered a few well-targeted assassinations of those who embodied the hope of this prosperous new world. With these assassinations, the people's will faltered. Their consciousness had been artificially expanded by ingesting narcotic substances. They soon returned to the status quo of fear and lies.

3

Eleanor

In London she was dying. Her spirit was damaged by her lover's betrayal. I met her at the Royal Botanic Gardens at Kew, in Greater London. She came to visit me in my wisteria temple home. Some of the branches of the wisteria were now more than six inches in diameter. It was in the shelter of the wisteria temple that she sat by me, the pale blossoms a shower of quiet blessings around us.

There is a time in one's life when the spirit is due to emerge. This is the essence of one's true self bringing to the world the gifts and talents previously locked in the soul before birth. It can be a dark time. Many turn back and return to their world of safety and logic, reason and fear. The uncertainty and doubts are as furies screaming profanities, taking the unsuspecting ones to the edge of sanity. The dark times are a temporary spiritual depression where one questions everything. It is a difficult time but ultimately rewarding for the strong hearted who learn to trust that guidance and support are always available.

My dark times have lasted many millennia but that has been my choice and mine alone. Eleanor was born to help my true self emerge and bring peace. No one seems to understand what peace means. Today, peace means an absence of war, but instead we have societies structured for violence in a different form: engineered material and spiritual poverty.

Before that day that I refuse to remember, peace was unbridled creativity, that brought prosperity in a finely tuned infrastructure of communities who trusted that any conflict could be resolved quickly to everyone's benefit. Resources were abundant because scarcity was seen as an illusion. It takes creativity and intelligence to make riches. My government was transparent. There was nothing to hide from my people.

Eleanor's creative energy was now awakening. By abandoning her faithless lover, she had embraced her destiny. I am part of that destiny. She does not know who I am, yet she knows herself even less. Eleanor has shown courage and strength sailing the stormy seas of uncertainty and doubt. Her heart is awakening so she will never be alone: she can now hear my voice through the darkness. I guide her by speaking to her from the stone tomb of my own heart. By healing Eleanor I heal myself.

A creative energy awakened is a potent weapon; it threatens those who need to control because they cannot express love. They seek to suppress those who dare to dream, otherwise they believe they cannot survive. This is a time of great fear but it is also a time of great compassion and awakening.

Eleanor had come to see me because she was homesick. She had come to live in a foreign land, leaving behind the memories of sadness in London. She would soon discover who she is destined to be, who she has always been. We can only discover who we are when we leave behind what we know. There is so much to tell. I am grateful for this time to speak. The Angel of Compassionate Condemnation watches over me. Roses are growing again at my plinth. Deep red, fragrant roses grow wherever I am placed. My caretakers at Kew did not understand this phenomenon. Some things are not meant to be analysed and explained but simply accepted. I cannot sense the fragrance nor can I touch the petals of soft velvet. They bud, bloom then shrivel away to rich rosehips while I remain unchanged and unchanging – an ancient soul in an ageless form of frozen beauty. The roses always come back anew. They taunt me with their life, their colour, their faith and fragile beauty.

I love them.

I hate them.

Eleanor, too, has a fragile beauty. She comes to spend time with me on her weekly visits to Golden Gate Park. There is so much to say, but I could see she was not ready to hear my voice until now. The relentless grey light of London in November can sap the soul but here, in the clear light of San Francisco in May, a new world can be born.

She sat askew on a curved marble bench to the right of my plinth. Eleanor faced west. The endless ocean and sky softened her heart and opened her mind. I faced east, inland, my heart insular.

'What is it that you fear?' I asked. Her heart was now open; I knew she could hear me.

'Wasting my life. Being on the wrong path.' Eleanor replied.

'No life is wasted. It is a law of the universe,' I said.

'Everything seems pointless.' she said. She stood so alone in a world of darkness and confusion. I wish she could see that many angels were around her at all times. Their guidance will flood through when her heart is filled with faith. Faith is not true or false, right or wrong; it is taking a stand for what will be. This is the meaning of, 'In the beginning was the word.'

'I am grateful to be here near you.' she said with a smile as though to temper the darkness in her soul. Gratitude is a powerful weapon against fear and uncertainty. She was no longer alone. She understood. Aurora flew over Eleanor's right shoulder in salute and Polaris cried out in delight high above us. The heavens work with us for our greater good. It is we who fight from fear. We can instead learn the law of allowing – that hidden path of serendipity where all things flow in perfect time and place. This is a divine right. Many lose sight of that path because their wounded souls have lost their connection to the heavens. We may spend lifetimes regaining that connection – a worthy quest.

Eleanor sat by me for a few minutes in quiet meditation. The caretakers at Kew had thoughtfully stipulated that a curved bench be placed a few feet from my plinth here at Golden Gate Park. Perhaps they had noticed my regular visitor. She grew serene before my eyes. It was nearly dusk, time for her to leave me and merge again into the vibrant bustle of the city beyond the park. I am never alone, yet without her I feel lonely. The mighty grace of the redwoods comfort me as the sun sets on this, a special day. Aurora and Polaris play in flight with the breezes from the ocean before they return to their perch for the night.

Dreams in stone are vivid and bright as the moon. Carrara-white marble glows in moonlight as it is a translucent stone. The memories are not so translucent. They are dark, deep in my being. Only a poet can set me free. Eleanor does not know who she is. She carries herself with the same demeanour, sedate and elegant; the same long flowing hair and the ageless beauty of someone soft and feminine yet firm and disciplined. She is Queen Eleni reborn. On that day that I refuse to remember, I had already killed her, not by my hands, but by my orders of assassination.

It was too late to rescind those orders when I had learned the error of my judgement. Her blood has stained my soul. The dreams return each night. They linger in the morning fog and are cleared away by sunshine at noon. I am clean and happy in sunshine; the sorrows of the world cannot touch me.

We live in a compassionate universe. Human beings create sorrow to relive the dramas of their ancestors. We relive their pain and sorrow to honour and love them. But then we visit our sorrows upon our children who are then born with the same imprinted memories. I see the same culture of lies and fear throughout the bloodiest of millennia. My enemy has been at work. His enforcers use the communications media to maintain the status quo of fear. The individual, according to him, must be kept separate, alone and above all, unable to think for him or herself. Whenever a creative idea for the empowerment of the self emerges, like a revolutionary film or an inspiring book, his agencies come forward to quash the credibility of the artists and scientists involved. My enemy's greatest fear is that humanity finds its own inner wisdom; those who are awakened in this way cannot be controlled by fear. His empires of wealth and influence are built on fear and lies.

4

XORAN/JAMES

A red glittering mist shrouds my eyes. Cold steel grips my heart and my chest tightens, stiffens, stops. The setting sun sends distant windows beyond the park into a rage of vermilion flashes, ephemeral jewels afire in concrete.

I breathe again.

I have a formidable adversary. I dare not underestimate him. Deceit and lies are weapons of spiritual damage deeper than any legendary sword. Losing the ability to trust another is sad; losing the ability to trust oneself is a tragedy. Destinies are marked by losses of trust for lifetimes. Souls are reborn to learn to trust once more. They learn to allow love to shine through the shadows of fear in the recesses of their hearts. I have returned to heal many damaged souls. Eleanor is the one I have come to protect. Through her, many will be healed.

His name is Xoran. That is his ancient name in a former lifetime. Today he is James Arthur Walter Shield III, born into a prominent old East Coast family with a legacy of fine schooling and business connections. The right secret society at an Ivy League college ensured him powerful connections for his objective of gaining maximum power with minimum accountability in Washington, DC. He is a master of the shadows, trusting no one but himself. If it were known, his judgement of human failings and weakness would be legendary. Mercifully, all records of my defeat by his trickery and deceit have been lost. My shame is now private, entombed in stone. Somewhere in this story I know it is necessary to heal my shame. The angels always say that not everything is as it seems. And so it is for me.

There is so much beauty. I cannot tell the beginning nor the end because I am the story unfolding still. It has been said that one cannot write the first line of a novel until the last line has been written. The story is revealed as an inscription in the author's heart, line by line. Each word is sacred when it is written, as though dictated from another realm beyond the material world. That is why only a poet can set me free. They hear with their hearts; they write from their souls.

Xoran or Mr James A. W. Shield III is a wealthy man. No, he seems to be wealthy; he is rich in financial resources but he has no true friends. His associates fear him. His subordinates crave admittance to his inner circle of power brokers though they never realise the price they pay. James hunts for human weakness in his counterparts before he considers committing any investment of time and money. Knowledge of that foible is power to him whether it be strange sexual practices or questionable transactions with a corrupt government department.

I do not wish to face him again. I shudder at the memory of his voice – a reptilian rasp betraying a life of privilege and entitlement but devoid of nobility. Shame freezes my heart yet I understand I must confront him once again. Each day I pray for strength and guidance.

'It is not Xoran you fear, my dear Clara,' said the Angel of Compassionate Condemnation. He shimmered in the low light of dusk. 'You cannot yet brave your own shadows of shame, locked in your being.'

'Am I doomed to watch him enslave the world once more?' I said.

'Soon you will be ready to do battle. The sacred warrior fights the shadows within. You have waited long and suffered much. The heavens were not aligned until now. The poet will fight alongside you. She was born for you.'

His words soothe me. I am not alone. The shimmering light softens and fades away but I am at peace. The trees darken against faint stars and the names begin again, one by one whispered on the wind through the leaves. To hear these names was once torture for me. Now they are my night-time prayers. Each name sacred. It takes three nights to hear all 50,000 names – a roll call of my sorrow? No, I have learned that those who died on that day I refuse to remember, each forgave me at the moment of their death. They had entered a contract before their birth that they were to die at my hand. It was I who would not forgive and so became stone.

The voices have always haunted me. They prayed for my freedom. I was too angry to understand, too rigid in my view to see their compassion. All I could hear was what seemed to be their condemnation. I was mistaken. I have learned late in life that everything is not always what it seems. We are in the closing years of a cycle in human history lasting 25,625 years – one galactic day – according to a calendar system familiar to my people. It is a time of great cataclysms and may seem to herald disaster for humanity. However, it is the rebirth of a great age where humans will follow the wisdom of their hearts, using their minds to service that wisdom. One of the greatest scientists of the twentieth century once said:

The intuitive mind is a sacred gift and the rational mind a faithful servant. We have created a society that honours the servant and has forgotten the gift.

A new pathway will become clear. That is my promise. First, I must defeat my enemy. He is poised to bring great terror and prevent humanity's transition to the great age. He feeds on their fear. The last five thousand years have been a most fruitful era for him in his many incarnations.

The twenty-first century since the birth of The Christ is a time when many established religions will fall. Those that advocate separation of humanity from their own inner wisdom will disappear. Those that serve their faithful will flourish in guiding them to their own divine consciousness. I know these are hard words. I am stone. The poet only needs to say the word and I shall be healed.

I do not know where Xoran, now known as James, is hiding. He will find me. I must wait even though Eleanor is in danger. Anger glows within me only as a faint memory. Since that day I refuse to remember, anger no longer burns through my veins but remains a memory frozen in shame.

I wait. I have waited before with a harder heart. Now my heart is human.

I felt a comforting presence, glowing brightly beside me.

'You have come far, my dear Clara,' the angel said. 'All has not been in vain. There is no need to fear.'

I could say nothing but shine in gratitude, the translucent stone trapping the sunlight dancing beneath the surface of my form. I have become a sacred prayer reverberating throughout my stone being. Now it begins. Do not pity me – I had created my own hell. On one plane of human consciousness, we are all statues, unable to face the deepest pain from our traumatic pasts. The body holds the tension in the tissues of the subconscious when the conscious mind cannot acknowledge the feelings themselves. I see many human statues every day. The children fill me with the greatest sorrow. They give up on their dreams so young and vulnerable. They believe the distorted limitations of their parents' world. Their heads hang low and their chests are sunken – the withdrawn hearts of those whose dreams have died, the handiwork of my enemy. His lies poison the very heart of humanity because the seeds of fear are planted so early. A child in the womb will hear and believe.

The light is always within.

This book is about the power of love, truth, and beauty, about finding our true centre instead of being tossed about on an ocean of lies. To know who we really are is our birthright.

5

Xavier/David

Eleanor arrived. So alive, so vital. How I envied her fluid movement. She sat down on the stone bench by my plinth and looked out towards the ocean.

'For a hundred years, I have watched beings in human form walk by me,' I said into her heart. 'In such a short time I have seen changes. People once bore their obligations on their shoulders, the weight crushing their hearts. Today, misery comes from an addiction to individual expression devoid of inner wisdom, purpose, and duty.'

'How can you tell?' said Eleanor.

'Shoulders were once rounded from their burdens. Today, the chest is sunken, the heart is pulled back and the head juts forward.' I said.

'What does it take to let go?' she asked.

'Growing beyond the pain – the sign of a soul growing and fully engaging the heart.' I found difficulty in speaking what I now understood through intuition but had never before expressed to another. 'To live fully, one needs a big, strong heart. Sometimes it is necessary to break open one's heart for it to grow.'

'Sounds dangerous,' she said. A cool afternoon breeze lifted a stray lock of dark hair across Eleanor's cheekbones. The wave of hair seemed a frayed flag flying at half-mast.

'Far more dangerous to play safe. Our true selves can be trapped within a hard capsule of false beliefs and fears. If we try to live by avoiding these lies, our hearts will give way to disease, our life force stifled.'

'I am broken but I am alive,' she said. 'Perhaps my heart is broken open too?'

'Trust your path. You shall soon be free.' My words landed in her soul. She arose, smiling, and walked back to her life in the city. She would soon meet Xavier's incarnation, David. I am filled with the joy of anticipation. How I have missed Xavier. His friendship and loyalty were the greatest of my treasures.

There is a rhythm to birth and death with many souls coming together in time for special missions on earth. There is a rhythm to reincarnation of soul ensembles. These are blessed beings who return to bring peace and enlightenment, lifetime after lifetime, during this five-thousand-year cycle of darkness. Xavier was reborn forty years ago as David – a man of honour, intelligence and integrity. He is now seasoned to a world of corruption but remains untouched and unscathed. I long to meet him in his present lifetime. We are now worlds apart but I will recognise the fire in his eyes as that of my loyal friend and chief of staff. I cannot embrace him. He does not know I now exist. That is my sadness, a grey hell. Soon he will meet Eleanor and my heart will leap with happiness out of my cold stone form. They will destroy my curse. A good soul never dies but simply finds a new vehicle for its next mission.

Death is a transformation I no longer fear. Instead, I fear wasting life in pursuit of meaningless trophies. Sometimes, I forget I have gained much in stillness, in learning, and in waiting. Sometimes, it would help to trust my own wisdom. The era of being a solitary witness will come to an end.

William waits for me. I will not fail him. My only brother followed me in my curse and waits for me in Kew, England. He is still there; a boulder of Botticino marble, a pale grey stone sculpted into the exquisite figure of an angel's head. He's placed near the Temperate House of the Royal Botanic Gardens. The rough surfaces of this marble figure are riven with veins of iron oxides weathered by soft English rain into rivers and pools of dried blood.

Eleanor was struck by his presence.

An adventurous soul is not an indulgent one. There is courage in facing the uncertain, the new. Coming to a new world has made Eleanor face her true self, not a surface self-patched together to conform to her native culture. We do not know who we really are until we are far from home. Trust in the stone. Gems are stone. They can guide us to who we truly are. We can choose the ones that are perfect for us. Each one holds its own vibration and powers. What if everything we do is perfect for where we are now? Statues have no time for judging others. We are too busy judging and condemning ourselves. That is why we are stone: we are alive but we do not live.

'Your mission is greater than you could ever foresee,' the angel spoke. It was dusk again. His shimmering light comforted me though his words did not.

'But what of Xavier's new incarnation, David?' The words breathed out of me. 'I owe him a heavy debt in this life.'

'Even though you took his life when he was Xavier, his soul willingly agreed to that destiny. It is for you to grant yourself forgiveness.' The angel faded into the dusk.

The stars reminded me that many worlds were watching tonight. The sky was far from lonely. The gentle chant of the names began again through the trees, and so did my sacred duty to listen until dawn.

My sacred duty was to listen. The angel's words resonated deep within me for many hours after his apparition faded. Each word became a mantra, some beyond the reach of my rational mind but always perfectly understood by my heart.

How does one forgive oneself?

I pray David will show me.

6

Eleanor and James

Eleanor placed her half-full champagne flute onto the tray held out by the waitress who moved with precision through the glittering throng of guests. Eleanor pulled the shimmering shawl over her bare shoulders. The silky fabric usually felt good against her skin. She usually felt good in her midnight-blue floor-length gown and elegant high heels. Instead, here, in the Jade Salon of the Walter Aston Hotel, she felt cold, almost naked. On instinct, she turned her head away from the gentleman approaching her. A flash of blue light refracted from the sapphire pendant at the base of her throat.

James was closer, two champagne flutes in hand. His smile disconcerted her.

Eleanor forced a smile and backed away ever so slightly. Her smile was as chilly as the champagne but without the effervescence. Her stance was a delicate balance of politeness and desire to flee.

'Pleasure to meet you, Ms Grey.' He offered her one flute of champagne.

'Thank you, Mr ...?' Eleanor accepted the glass graciously and regained her balance.

'James Shield III at your service,' he replied.

'Pleasure to meet you too, Mr Shield,' Eleanor lied.

'Call me James.' He clinked his glass to hers while keeping a respectful physical distance. 'You certainly stand out from the crowd. Let's have dinner tomorrow.'

'I'd love to, James, but I'm heading back to San Francisco in the morning,' Eleanor lied again. She took a cautious sip of champagne, the crystal glass cold against her lower lip. She wasn't leaving New York until the day after tomorrow but she had little desire to share her true itinerary with this man. 'What brings you here this evening?' she asked, even though she already knew the answer: another suave government type from one of the myriad national security agencies, replete with the required prosaic acronym, seeking to interfere with and manipulate the non-profit's cash flow.

'The board invited me some time ago,' James lied also. 'I'm here to help,' he added. His face had a soft expression of synthetic solemnity that men like him have practised very well. He then stood a little closer. Eleanor raised her head to look up at his face but avoided looking into his eyes. She did not know he had met with a couple of board members earlier this week. When he'd mentioned the non-profit's tax-exempt status could be fragile, the board members viewed James in a sudden, more favourable light. He was at the fundraising event to hold further informal meetings with the board of directors, seeking to use their infrastructure, of course. Non-profit organisations may be used to camouflage clandestine funding of unexplained and unacknowledged activities overseas.

James kissed Eleanor's cheek. A kiss gentle of touch but firm of intent. His right cheekbone brushed against hers. A gesture swift but sure. Eleanor stood, dumbfounded, overwhelmed by his presence. His skin had an acrid, leathery, almost animal scent. The muskiness chilled her body to the bone in an irrational, impossible recognition. The mask of his expensive sandalwood, vanilla and lavender cologne did not fool her body's wisdom.

Eleanor did not know that James was accustomed to getting what he wanted. Her earlier stance, polite though standoffish, only further intrigued and aroused him. She was beyond the bounds of his control. Other women, excited by his power and influence, were only too eager to ingratiate themselves with him, proffering their business cards along with their breasts in a soft, yearning body stance while standing too close to him and staring too hard into his eyes. These women had no idea how they bored men like James. Their need to validate their insecure feminine selves repelled him. Eleanor did not know how to behave that way. She was always her own person and treated everyone with kindness and respect.

'Your scent is quite captivating,' James said.

'Oh, James,' Eleanor replied, her voice uncharacteristically shrill, 'maybe it's the champagne. I really don't feel well.' Eleanor stepped back away from James, with a slight stagger. Behind her, a jade-green marble-clad pillar with a huge palm provided some shelter. 'Or it could be jetlag,' she added.

'May I accompany you to your hotel?' James was concerned. As a seasoned traveller he knew flying east across even just three time zones could cause problems.

'Thank you, that won't be necessary. I have a car waiting.' Eleanor continued the pretence. 'Please excuse me.' She placed the champagne flute on a tray on a side table and glided between the other guests to the ladies' rest room past the foyer.

James followed but waited for Eleanor at the coat check.

Eleanor appeared a few minutes later. Her face flushed slightly at seeing James.

'Allow me to accompany you to your car,' he offered. Eleanor retrieved her evening coat from the coat-check attendant.

'Thank you. That's very kind,' Eleanor replied as James helped her with her coat. She was relieved he was not standing too close this time. The musky scent was not so overpowering. She had already called the chauffeur on his mobile phone. He was bringing the town car to the hotel's side entrance in a few minutes.

Outside the hotel, James held open the town car's rear passenger door for Eleanor.

'Are you sure you cannot have dinner with me tomorrow night?' James asked. He gave her a pleasant smile.

'I am afraid not. Perhaps another time.' Eleanor smiled back at James. He stood facing her and was about to step closer again. She was about to lose her nerve. Was there no escape? Was he ever going to let her go? Married men like him were always so direct and demanding in pursuing other women. Single men never seemed to have the same focus and determination.

With her back against the open car door, she bent her knees, slipped onto the car seat backwards, gathered her gown, and swung her feet up and into the car's spacious footwell. James smiled at her elegant manoeuvre. He ensured the hems of Eleanor's coat and gown were clear and reluctantly closed the car door. He stepped back from the kerb and smiled once more at Eleanor.

Eleanor fastened her seatbelt. 'I'm ready. Please drive,' she instructed the chauffeur and breathed a sigh of relief as the town car pulled away from the hotel.

Eleanor did not know what it was about him she found so disturbing. I, Clara, would gladly enlighten her but she was not yet ready.

Little did she know, though she escaped him this time, James would have her watched: standard operating procedure in all his affairs, business or otherwise, where someone always gets screwed but rarely James himself. In his former incarnation as King Xoran, James was accustomed to using, abusing, and discarding young beautiful women abducted from their villages in lieu of taxes.

I wish I could warn my friend and protect her. It is hard at times to let those I love find their own way. But find their own way they must.

7

THE SWORDS: CLARITY AND BRILLIANCE

~ Clara ~

I had lived by these swords. It was therefore fitting to die by them. My clarity of mind and brilliance of being had faded long before my death. The blood flowed hot with the bright steel blade of Clarity driven deep into my solar plexus. The walnut-sized violet diamond in the pommel darkened as my body bled into the ground.

It was a good death: swift and clean. I was at peace. Hell did not frighten me: I had already condemned my soul for an eternity.

The swords are lost to time. Eleanor is the rightful steward of their power. They do not remain in the possession of those who are unworthy. An ancient curse breathes through the steel forged under the auspices of Archangel Michael himself. King Xoran had seized them at my death, along with their bejewelled scabbards, but they later disappeared from his campaign headquarters leaving no trace. In his anger he ordered the summary execution at dawn of all guards on duty that night.

No one said prayers over their pyres. Their souls remained trapped on earth.

My once clear mind was clouded with fear while the brilliance of my being was dulled by doubt. I believed there was no one I could trust. Xoran had played his game well. He was the sole victor in the game of statecraft while I was one of the million vanquished. He conquered by creating and enforcing a state of fear where distrust of each other and of oneself was the normal accepted way of life. There can be no enduring prosperity in such a climate, because there is no place for the most fundamental of human virtues: a passionate desire to serve a greater good.

I did not live to see my empire die. I was spared the sadness of watching communities of prosperous merchants and traders weaken in the regime of corrupt government officials. Not only could my people no longer trust each other, but all resources that were once abundant, like fresh spring water, became scarce. The sadness followed me into my death. Corruption thrived in deliberate confusion and neglect bred more fear. I had caused the essence of evil to be manifest among my people.

I miss my swords. They were a potent symbol that galvanise the spirit. They reminded me where to wield my tremendous hidden powers. Symbols are potent when they represent the same qualities already within.

Clarity and brilliance are qualities possessed by all. Every person fears not their shadows, but their unique brilliance. Despite my wisdom and intelligence, I had made a mistake and my people paid the price: I chose to ignore my intuition and instead I believed the lies that poisoned my imperial court. To believe is simply to pledge my allegiance to a point of view. Nothing was real until I made a choice, until I chose a point of view. My reality changed according to how I perceived it. Where there was once joy, had become terror.

Forgive me, the years in stone have been lonely and the pain in my heart profound. If I could make sense of the pain then maybe it would cease, but I have learned that is a fantasy typical of a statue. Pain flows in waves as the body-mind heals. The rational mind believes it can use logic to control the pain. Logic is a fallacy, a distraction from the deeper awakening of the heart.

I cannot express the depths of my love for Queen Eleni who is now Eleanor. She will soon meet Xavier who is now David. I miss my friend Xavier. They both forgave me at the very moment of their deaths. My heart cannot accept such generosity of spirit – I had murdered these two magnificent beings. My own healing is slow but steadfast.

There are sacred words known only by a few people blessed with wisdom. The words heal when they are spoken. We may see ourselves as a prayer embodied. Each one of us is a prayer destined to heal another. Listen carefully and you will hear the prayer you were born to be. This story is my prayer. I thank you from the depths of my being for sitting with me these few short hours.

Aurora shrieks with joy. Eleanor approaches again on foot through the park in the afternoon sunshine. Aurora swoops down, her two-and-half-metre wingspan grazes Eleanor's sunhat. The hat falls to the side of the path and Eleanor's long dark hair dances in the turbulent wake of the eagle's wings.

'How lovely to see you again, Aurora!' Eleanor picks up her hat, smiling, and looks upwards, shielding her eyes from the sun using her hand as a visor. The golden eagle soars higher, buoyed by the warm afternoon breeze, a crooked feather fluttering on her left wing.

'Good day, Eleanor.' I breathe the words so they land in her heart. 'Please find my swords.'

8

THE DAY I REFUSE TO REMEMBER — 25,000 YEARS AGO

~ Clara ~

This was the real beginning of time as understood today in the twenty-first century since the birth of the one called Christ. All knowledge was lost in the many destructive wars of the past five thousand years. All knowledge of who we really are, who we can be, is concealed in mystery overlaid with impenetrable sheaths of enforced ignorance.

Ten years before the day I refused to remember, I was a student, a young woman, enrolled in The Academy of The Sacred Warrior. Our tutors were enlightened beings who taught us that true battles lie within and that we are all one. They came from many worlds beyond mine. My fellow students were drawn from many lands in the empire, irrespective of rank, race, creed, or gender. The only required qualities were a quick intuitive mind and a courageous heart.

My favourite classes were sword mastery and equestrian battle skills. I struggled with both of these classes at first. Both were taught by kind Andromedans of indeterminate age. They would smile at my impatience to master specific stances and techniques. They would remind me to still my adolescent mind and allow my body to learn the movements as a form of meditation in motion. Too much thinking, too much anxiety would cloud my progress. I soon learned to be in tune with both horse and sword. I later learned the true purpose of these classes was to discipline and strengthen my mind as well as my physical body to guard our peaceful world. I later learned my Andromedan tutors were many centuries of age. The tutor of sacred mathematics, an Arcturian, was more than a thousand years old. I grew to love geometry and astronomy because of her wit and wisdom.

It was hard to sustain enmity with foreign peoples when conflicts were defused long before they grew to be a danger to our people. We learned ways to understand ourselves and be open to the ways of many different peoples. We protected our country as sacred warriors with wisdom and compassion, power and grace. Lethal force had no utility unless there was a clear outcome where all parties eventually win. The finest warriors rarely resorted to lethal force.

Some students did not complete the training. The shadows in their hearts proved too strong to penetrate in their present lifetime. Or the training was not their true path. The tutors released these students to serve a role more fulfilling for them in society. There was no shame, only love and appreciation for the individual gifts and talents discovered. By following a path that led to apparent failure, the student found a path closer to their true calling.

Eleanor understands this in her soul, but at the present time her mind obstructs the way. It has been conditioned by the concerns of the external world. Only the internal world is worth heeding. Eleanor's healing is rapid. Soon, she will be clear, her mind transparent and resilient. Her mind will serve her heart, instead of dominating and stifling its quiet guidance. My mind, once rigid and rational, must first become open and flexible, accepting new points of view. Seasons of psychosis and depression are usual at this time. My entire being adjusts to the higher energy frequency of my awakened heart. The dark depression, confusion, and doubt are simply the shadows in my heart being dispelled by the swords of light. My swords will find Eleanor. It will not be a difficult mission for them: the swords chose her long before she was born.

There is a rhyme and a reason to the seasons of my madness. My awakening heart will release my mind from the virus of fears, lies, restrictive beliefs, and fixed ideas underlying my society. In regaining my sanity, it may seem, to the unenlightened, that I have gone quite mad.

Being a statue is to witness the dreams of some turn to dust while those of others are realised. To pursue my dream means to disobey fearful thoughts and to lovingly disregard anyone who says my dreams are impossible. These are almost impossible acts for a statue yet my heart yearns to transcend my limitations.

I long for my horses. I used to ride like the wind with Andromeda – a tall black Arabian, a big-hearted trusty mare. At a gallop her long mane was a dancing black wave. She was with me that day. Her whinny of distress faded from my senses; the sound dislocated inside me to some far dimension. She stood firm by my body as consciousness bled from me on that battlefield. Andromeda will be with me again one day. That is my dream.

I have another dream: Richard will ride alongside me again, just as we once did after daily equestrian class at the Academy. He grew to become my field commander and my love. He was assassinated before that battle. The news of betrayal damaged morale in my forces. I ordered Richard's adjutant to be tortured. I signed those orders. The seemingly faithless man was protecting his young family held prisoner by Xoran. He had betrayed his beloved commanding officer under duress. I could not hear the adjutant's screams from behind the marble and silks of my private palatial apartments but his blood, too, stains my soul. I had chosen to believe the lies.

There was no turning back. My chief of staff, Xavier, had been reported to be in conspiracy with Queen Eleni of the Realm of Light. Her troops were marching across into our territory. We had no garrison in that area. There was never any reason to deploy forces where there were no enemies. Without Richard or Xavier, I acted in haste, blinded without the ones I trusted the most. I had not received despatches in days. My messenger eagles, the fastest on earth, were missing.

I ordered a unit of my secret guard to seek out and assassinate both Xavier and Queen Eleni. I joined my late commander's unit and marshalled our forces to engage Queen Eleni's troops approaching us from the east. My scouts reported that the foreign troops were a small division in single column and in ceremonial dress. I interpreted this information as trickery and ordered an attack at first light. My brother, William, was to remain behind as I instructed. He was still too young to see battle.

My scouts were correct. Queen Eleni's troops were, as reported, lightly armed and escorting what appeared to be tributes and gifts. Only one thousand souls. More trickery. On my signal, my forces slaughtered them all. I held the sword Clarity high and lowered it to the side of my boot in one flashing movement, unleashing hell. Andromeda remained still but I could feel her adrenaline – the smell of fear and fresh blood leaves no one untouched.

A courier rode fast towards me surprising my guards into attack, but I recognised him as one of Xavier's staff and allowed him to approach me. I do not know why. His expression was strange and grey. He asked me to accompany him to another part of the battlefield. I took a detachment with me and followed him.

A young male was laid out on the grass, wrapped in my father's purple cloak. This was part of my father's battledress and had not been seen in battle since his death ten years earlier. I dismounted. Fell to my knees beside the adolescent. William was dying in my arms. I held him, my sweet brother, my light, until the light behind his eyes departed. I held him, still warm, still alive in my heart, but he was gone. There was a scream inside me that stopped at my chest. My voice gone, singing him a lullaby in a cracked falsetto.

I rose to my feet. My legs were unsteady and seemed disconnected from the earth. I was a ghost. Another courier arrived on horseback, this time carrying documents covered in dried blood. One of my missing messenger eagles had reached a nearby camp. She was wounded, and died delivering a preliminary alliance treaty of prosperity between my realm and The Realm of Light, signed by Queen Eleni. A covering note from Xavier explained the innocent venture and exonerated them both. A surprise for my birthday celebrations early next month. The troops in ceremonial dress were indeed bringing tributes to me. The message had been delayed by fourteen days. Just enough time to create confusion and doubt. It was too late to rescind my orders of assassination. Xavier and Queen Eleni were already dead.

William was killed by an advance guard from Xoran's forces which had been in pursuit all along. William was a prime target. The purple cloak, richly embroidered in gold, heralded his identity from afar. My poor, foolish, valiant brother. Xoran's troops overwhelmed us all.

A fiery glimmer. A red glow before me. The afternoon sun struck the large cabochon ruby in Xoran's belt and flashed against his cuirass, cuisse, and greaves. His armour shone untainted as though he had not drawn blood in this battle.

He was on horseback – his usual grey Arabian. The horse snorted, pranced about, dark eyes wide open, ringed in white. The blue-violet flash of the violet diamond in Clarity's pommel faded to dark grey. The sword was in me now.

Haemorrhage was so warm. Effortless.

Peace.

'Bring me the head, the swords, the scabbards, and the horse. Leave the bitch to rot.' Xoran did not dismount but gave orders while pointing his sword. The comet Aurelius streamed overhead, so bright it was visible in daylight. He looked up, squinted, and smiled at the blazing tail that stretched across the sky. Little did he know the comet that foretold his victory today would one day foretell his doom.

Xoran's adjutant, a captain, untied the scabbards and took both swords, still glowing, from my corpse. When he withdrew Clarity from my bleeding chest, both swords became heated and scorched the captain's hands through his gauntlets. He winced hard and stifled a scream that surged from his chest. He dropped the swords. They clinked, clanked, and sang to the ground. The captain unhooked my cloak and used it to wrap the swords instead.

Xoran's retinue took my head away, but that is of no consequence. My soul was lost. I invoked The Angel of Compassionate Condemnation. He answered and came to my side.

That is all I care to remember.

9

WHO AM I?

~ Clara ~

I became stone. My heart remained closed for millennia. That was only my physical being. My spirit yearns to soar. My fears fade but dangers mount.

I beseech the gods and my Angel of Compassionate Condemnation for strength and clarity. My mind assumes I lacked the qualities and abilities to complete the mission before me, that I am somehow insufficient in myself to succeed. The angel tells me these are common illusions created by the human mind conditioned in a climate of fear.

Deep in my heart I feel the true wealth of experience and skill lying dormant within me. Difficult circumstances and obstacles challenge me to unearth my hidden gifts and talents. Here, faith is creativity, strength, and courage. I pray for this faith to suffuse my stone being.

There is beauty in stone; as a statue, an unchanging ageless appearance is a gift but it is also my curse. Sunlight dances on the translucent layers beneath the surface of white marble so beautiful as though from the famed quarries of Carrara in Italy. I glow in the light of the full moon but I pray to live again as vibrant flesh and bone.

I pray for a heavenly death.

I succeeded my father at too young an age. He died after a brief illness. Dark secrets lay like fault lines across the foundations of the imperial court. No one dared ask questions. I always suspected foul play but did nothing to prove or disprove my suspicions for fear of arousing powerful enemies. I wished to protect my brother, William.

I failed.

The secrets and the lies poisoned me. My mind rationalised endlessly: it sought to find reasons to believe the lies. But my heart always knew the truth. My body and my spirit paid the price.

I wish Richard were by my side, both of us alive in each other's arms. Our souls land gently, returning to our bodies still entwined, spent, and tumescent with showers of grace in the ecstasy of our union. He has been searching for me for thousands of years in every incarnation since his assassination in our last lifetime together. Every time he incarnated he thought he had found me when he fell in love. But the woman he was seeking never did reincarnate. He did not know I had been stone for many millennia. I grieve that he suffered so long because of my curse. I have always loved him. Even in stone there is no respite. The yearning aches through my being.

I dare to experience desire and longing. It is a sign of new life within me but brings me much pain. Stone once protected me from the pain of awakening, but now it imprisons my soul.

I committed acts of evil.

Unspeakable acts have been committed under my orders.

During my thousands of years in stone I failed to understand what happened. I failed to comprehend the deeds I committed when I was in human form. At last, in the last five thousand years, the age of destruction, my failings became clear to me. I had chosen to believe the lies of fear. I could see successive wars were always preceded by greed, fear, and lies in corrupt government institutions just like my mine. The lifespan of human beings shortened in this dark age. The corrosive effect of stress hormones – degraded lands, foul air, and dirty waters – aged the human body rapidly within a mere seventy years or less. Before that day I refused to remember, humans lived full active lives of five or six centuries.

The Angel of Compassionate Condemnation stands near me as always. He comforts me with news that this age of destruction will soon end. Only one person stands in the way of our planetary transformation:

Xoran or, as he is known today, James.

10

THE WAY OF LIES

~ Clara ~

There is a saying in England: where there's a will, there's a way. I failed to learn in my last lifetime that if my will was aligned with my heart, my life would have been filled with grace; those beautiful synchronicities where my needs would have been met with ease.

I learned only in the last few centuries, with the angel's patient guidance, that surrendering my will to the divine is not weakness as in the way of my ego. Surrender is the way of the wise, allowing divine will to flow through my physical being.

Not my will, but thy will be done on earth as it is in heaven.

At first I feared the uneasy feeling in my stone form, conditioned to the supremacy of my rational mind. The angel promised me that an aliveness and a passion would emerge beyond concerns for my needs and goals in themselves alone. Standing for a grander purpose for the greater good of our world, our planet, now strengthens my aliveness.

I could have hidden myself in stone for an eternity. I could have avoided making any choices and avoided any responsibility for them. However, the angel warned me those who stand for nothing, fall for anything.

I had lost sight of my grander purpose and became enmeshed in avoiding the political squabbles in my court following my father's death. With the constant threat from King Xoran of the Land of Shadows, my imperial throne was weakened by spies and sabotage. I made many mistakes in my desire to protect my brother William until he was old enough to rule. I had no wish for imperial office, but I had a duty to succeed my father. My beloved mother died soon after my father's death. Heartbreak was the cause, I was told.

William and I were alone.

Xavier was our confidante and advisor. He could always be distinguished from his twin, Xoran, by the fluid discipline of his gait. Xavier's scent was a subtle cedar and sandalwood blend, the scent of trust. Xoran was the exact same height, build, and colouring as his brother. They shared the same facial features, but Xoran moved with stiffness, his scent acrid and bitter beneath the expensive blend of civet, castoreum, frankincense, and myrrh. Xavier radiated beauty and goodness in his smile while Xoran could force a brilliant smile but his face was grey and his eyes glistened – a gaze brittle and cold.

The body never lies. A person may say words that mean little, but the body always betrays real intent. I did not understand this in my innocence. I believed the lies and rumours in my court about Xavier's loyalty. When his gait stiffened, his dress more ostentatious than usual, his scent no longer pleasant but bitter, I began to doubt him too. I discovered too late that Xoran had been impersonating my friend, creating doubt and confusion throughout my court. I believed the doubt and confusion to be real. I chose the Way of Lies and paid a heavy price.

Xavier had left long ago to visit Queen Eleni in the Realm of Light to negotiate a treaty for mutual security, prosperity and peace. They also wished to declare their intention to marry. They sought my blessing and in return the Realm of Light would unite with the Empire of Peace.

The whispers of a beloved forever haunt my guilty heart. It was easier to become stone to control the pain, easier to stop breathing and depart the body. The living hell I had created could not be escaped by mere death. Fiery anger and self-loathing filled my soul while it dislocated from my body as it cooled on that battlefield, on that day.

Becoming stone was my salvation. From one hell to another, to escape the conflagration of emotion within me. There was no escape; until I faced my failings there could be no true salvation. The angels could only guide and encourage me. My free will decides my fate. I had surrendered my will many millennia past, not to the divine, but to an intractable fear.

I am soon to confront my enemy and, in doing so, I confront the woman I was so long ago: that misguided, naïve fool, a disgrace to my family's noble lineage.

'Healing begins with forgiveness,' said the Angel of Compassionate Condemnation, 'Release the suffering of past actions. The lessons were powerful and you have mastered the learning.' His deep voice resonated through me. His angel title may seem strange. Heaven never condemned me but sent an angel to my aid, to defeat the shadows of my self-condemnation. In that darkness I may discover the light of my soul. That light may navigate me out of the stormy Way of Lies to the way of my highest truth, the one locked in my heart.

Today, I dream each day in stone that Xavier and Eleni may meet again. I know they will in this, their present, lifetimes. It is their destiny. Even though I had thwarted the fulfilment of their love, my heart fills with the joy of anticipation. Rigid structures like stone cannot take too much joy. Almost invisible cracks dull the translucence of my marble being. Joy is life force manifest; a continual unfolding and growth, transforming old ways to reveal one's highest destiny.

Old structures break down as a butterfly discards its chrysalis.

My desire is that everyone on Earth discovers the way of their highest truth.

It is possible.

So be it.

11

MY DAYS

~ Eleanor ~

I left London and came to San Francisco. An irresistible job opening: I was employed by the investment firm of a wealthy family. I spent my days analysing stock market data and balance sheets of business concerns in the USA. I even did a little financial market trading of my own. It appealed to my orderly and analytical mind to maintain logs and spreadsheets of my profits and losses when I followed the trending prices of the British Pound Sterling against the United States Dollar.

In London, I had studied an intense course that trained me in spotting opportunities in financial markets. As markets are run by human beings and trading algorithms there are always cyclical shifts in prices that form patterns in price charts, revealing opportunities with advance signals. With skill and discipline, a trader can see these signals and take appropriate action with minimal downside risk.

I always found comfort and a strange satisfaction in the precision of trading currencies – a global twenty-four-hour financial market. My romantic relationships, meanwhile, were fraught with fear. I had to leave London. The city suffocated me with memories of the former boyfriend in every building, every bridge, every street corner, every bus, train, Tube, and taxi. In San Francisco I could breathe. Even the fog was a soft balm for my broken heart. It would be some time before I returned to the city of my birth. It would be some time, if ever, before I fell in love again.

How could heartbreak make me question everything? The pain seared through every belief I once held inviolate. Sitting with my thoughts and demons was torture. Far better to throw myself into intense but meaningless activity: I worked at a demanding job for money with no benefit for humanity. At least this meaningless job afforded me the opportunity to live and work in a beautiful city five thousand miles from my former home.

San Francisco was my home now. My heart healed with the gentle turn of each California season.

One step at a time.

I took one step in life before the next step was revealed. Gone were the days when I could be sure, when I could look ahead to a life of romance and passion. What a fool I was. I was stupid to believe in him when the evidence came up short. Why did love make me blind? Did I need that mediocre romance so much? Was I willing to ignore the quiet voice in my heart and compromise my soul? There were whispers of discontent within me. There were gentle warnings I failed to heed: his intense stare at a tall, lanky Swedish waitress at a restaurant early in our relationship. If I had listened, I would not have been in such pain.

I was my own worst enemy.

Today, I stand on the brink of engagement in a new battle of love. An attractive gentleman has been stalking me. His demeanour seems without menace. I have not confronted him. I have enjoyed what seems to be his protective presence. I do not know where an encounter would lead. I only trust that I can manage any situation that may arise.

My head aches again around the temples, needles of pain along my hairline. Clara said the pain indicates an awakening: a rigid mind and a closed heart becoming open, fluid, and vibrant. I have never been any good at living with uncertainty and setbacks. They would usually plunge me into the grey sea of depression.

Clara saved me.

In England, I would sit on the bench by her plinth in the wisteria gazebo at the Royal Botanic Gardens, Kew. The serenity of her marble form would calm the turmoil in my heart. An hour in meditation would pass as though only a minute. I would leave refreshed and happier than when I arrived.

One day, Clara disappeared from Kew.

I was bereft.

I tracked her down: she had been transferred to Golden Gate Park. A few months later, I moved to San Francisco.

12

GRACE CATHEDRAL PART I

Eleanor visits Grace Cathedral in San Francisco on Thursday afternoons. In this house of prayer for all people she prays for me. David has been watching her. He was sent by James.

For weeks, David has observed her innocuous life. His distaste for the assignment was tempered by a growing fascination for his target, James's prey. David had never before seen a woman so self-contained, so regal yet unassuming in her demeanour. She was quiet but not shy. He longed to discover what thoughts lay behind the serene glow in her face and the smooth purpose in her gait. James gave him only the facts: Eleanor Alice Grey, forty-four years old, single, no children, recently arrived from London, lives in Berkeley, works in San Francisco's financial district between Market and California Streets.

Facts alone are like bones – lifeless without the flesh of story.

David's daily challenge was to concoct reports of her activities that would pique his employer's interest back in Washington, DC, without incriminating her, and so prolong his assignment. He wanted to be near her but he was running short of stories and ideas. He needed to approach her soon.

He did not understand the purpose of his mission. As usual, details were only released on "a need-to-know-basis" – the clumsy jargon of his employer, an unacknowledged department headed by James A. W. Shield III within the United States Department of Defense.

If you knew your way around government accounting and audit rules, it was possible to do anything with government approval. With his network of contacts in government and among defence contractors, James wielded disproportionate influence in government: power without public accountability. Xoran gained such expertise from his many lifetimes across twenty-five millennia to his present incarnation, James.

David Xavier Feraud had been an investigative journalist in Washington, DC who upset too many powerful officials in pursuing stories of government corruption. He was betrayed by an associate who had passed him fabricated evidence. An embarrassing retraction of a story by his newspaper preceded his downfall. His public stance was, if you can't beat them, join them. His private attitude was another matter. When James's department offered him a lowly researcher position, David accepted. James liked to keep his enemies close, especially if they were useful.

David watched Eleanor and became enchanted by her. He had access to government surveillance technology that tracked credit cards, bank accounts, and her telephones, both her office line and mobile phone. He searched and watched for a significant masculine presence in her life, but there was none. The more he watched, the more of a mystery she became.

One afternoon, as usual, he tracked her to Golden Gate Park. He made sure to remain just out of sight as Eleanor walked past the California Academy of Sciences towards the San Francisco Botanical Garden. Today he was disguised as a park gardener rather than a botanical researcher or nature photographer. Eleanor seemed oblivious to his existence. His heart felt heavy at the thought of never becoming a part of her life, but he quickly brought himself under control. His mission was to track and report, not follow and engage in flirty conversation.

Discipline. Stay focused. Stay out of sight.

Eleanor slowed down and stopped for a moment. She turned and looked around then seemed to take her time to continue on her path. She crossed Martin Luther King Drive and entered the botanical garden by the North gate reserved for San Francisco Botanical Garden members. He gained entry soon after Eleanor with his new membership pass. Last time he followed Eleanor, he could not enter at her usual gate but had to use the main gate on Lincoln Drive and lost her.

The gentle perfume from the many flowers in bloom along the borders of the path almost hypnotised him. He kept a steady distance behind her, about a hundred metres at least.

The cool breeze and warm sunshine made Eleanor seem more vivid yet even more out of reach.

Eleanor stopped before an unusual white stone statue: an intricate sculpture of a tall majestic woman, a surreal beauty enrobed in regal garments and armed with two magnificent swords. Statues of feminine forms in a botanical garden would usually be half- or fully naked, representing the beauty of the natural world. This statue Eleanor visited represented something else entirely yet the statue seemed perfectly situated. He had advanced closer and kept watch through his camera lens from behind dense fragrant shrubs. David was not sure if it was just the afternoon sunshine striking the surface of the pale stone, but the statue seemed to glow and become more luminous as Eleanor approached.

Eleanor sat down on a curved stone bench by the statue and gazed up at the statue's face. She sat still, peaceful.

An hour passed.

She rose from the bench, looked up at the statue again, smiled, and walked away, taking the same path back through the botanical garden and the park.

David wondered why she visited a statue in Golden Gate Park. When he first sent photos of these visits to James, David was puzzled by his employer's heated interest in both the statue and Eleanor. The investigative part of his mind awakened. He needed to tread with care; he wanted to uncover the real story without endangering Eleanor.

The statue in Golden Gate Park would give off a luminous glow in Eleanor's presence. The difference was noticeable, especially on those grey foggy days typical of some summer days in San Francisco. The glow would fade as Eleanor walked away.

She also would spend time at Grace Cathedral in, what seemed to David, quiet contemplation. He did not know why.

On another day, David followed Eleanor into the cathedral. He watched her walk to the icon of Sophia in the western chapel, the altar of sacred feminine wisdom. There, Eleanor would spend time in prayer. He did not want to watch her in such a sacred place but waited outside on the cathedral steps. He was entranced by the labyrinth meditation circle in the cathedral plaza.

The circle was about forty feet in diameter, laid in a pale and a dark shade of grey terrazzo stone that marked a swirling, convoluted path within the circle. The path would guide a meditator through a twenty-minute walk in the labyrinth, exiting alongside the point of entry. One slow walk without tricks or dead ends. The urgent rumble of motor traffic and clatter of cable cars sounding their tinny bell on Nob Hill would fade into a muffled world of far less importance.

'Defies logic, doesn't it?' she said.

He could not speak for a second. A beat of his heart. He turned to face the mysterious voice behind him.

'It's beautiful. What's it for?' he said. He smiled at that familiar face.

'A thirteenth-century meditation exercise that silences the mind and connects you to your divine self. The circle's a copy of one in France.' A gentle smile shone through Eleanor's eyes. David glowed, warm from mild perspiration.

'I'm David.' He extended his hand in handshake.

'I take it you already know my name.' She surrendered her hand into his. David held it a fraction too long. Her hand felt soft in his, but her handshake felt firm as though vibrant steel in velvet.

13

Grace Cathedral Part II

Eleanor stared out of her twentieth-floor office window. She was seated, left elbow on the desk near the keyboard. She propped up her chin in the palm of her left hand, fingers curled under her lower lip. Her right hand played with a mouse device, and a cursor wandered unsupervised across all three computer screens. Her focus softened into the distance. The familiar neighbouring towers in San Francisco's financial district seemed busier than normal. The Transamerica Pyramid pierced the sky. Spring, so far, had been overcast, the gloom heavy, but for the first time in weeks, clouds cleared to reveal blue, beautiful blue.

Eleanor brought her focus back to the screens on her desk. A soft sigh escaped from her chest. She hated working on these quarterly reports: her employer wanted an analysis of lowest-quartile-performing stocks to detect any previously hidden opportunity for investment or company turnaround.

The usually bloated numbers were the ratio of executive compensation versus median employee salary. Whereas the usually skinny numbers were the proportion of women in senior management even when the majority of employees were female. The environmental, social, and governance indicators were absent or suitably greenwashed.

Eleanor sensed the narrow and stunted consciousness of the companies in her quarterly report just by examining their numbers.

On occasion, she saw an improvement in a company's performance not shown in operating profits or sales turnover but evident in another indicator: a possible investment opportunity. Nothing was guaranteed, of course. Some improvements were short-lived as the entrenched company culture of greed and mismanagement kept the company in mediocrity. Some companies later filed for bankruptcy.

Eleanor was mindful of companies showing unusually high profits with no apparent cause, and treated their numbers with caution. She remembered hearing the story of Crazy Arnie and The Panama Pump in an accounting course at college. Arnie Safdieh owned a chain of discount electronics stores across New York, New Jersey, and Connecticut in the 1970s and 1980s. He skimmed profits for years via Tel Aviv and later "pumped" the cash back into the business via bank accounts in Panama when the company went public in 1984. The company seemed to be raining cash to unwary stock market investors. Shares traded at a few dollars on its initial public offering and later peaked nearly ten times higher. Arnie Safdieh and some of his family members made millions of dollars from selling their shares at inflated prices. He eventually served eight years in prison for racketeering.

Her head was aching from staring at spreadsheets too long. Nothing on the screens made sense. Numbers danced up and down and back and forth across the many columns and rows of her intricate spreadsheets that she affectionately named her Crazy Arnie Files.

Eleanor pressed two keys on the keyboard. Her workstation was now suspended and locked. She picked up her handbag and her suit jacket, but left the pair of elegant flat shoes under her desk. She walked to the elevators, navigating the maze of clear and frosted glass walls of meeting rooms and her colleagues' offices.

Outside the building, Eleanor walked on the sidewalk through a shaft of sunlight that burst from an alleyway between two granite-faced buildings. She felt better already. Usually, she walked east towards the Embarcadero, but today she desired something else. She headed north on Montgomery, turned left onto California Street, and walked at a steady pace up the hill. She let her mind wander and walked one mindful step at a time.

Eleanor's mind became quieter and clearer with every step. After walking three blocks along California Street, the incline steepened and her feet began to ache. A distant tinny bell sounded behind her and was getting closer. Fifty feet ahead of her was the California and Stockton cable-car stop. The clanging and clattering car arrived at the stop at the same time as she did on foot. Eleanor rode the cable car up the hill. At California and Jones, the majesty of Grace Cathedral came into view and she stepped off the car as soon as it stopped.

That masculine presence was there again, but something about it seemed reassuring, almost protective. Eleanor was not sure. In any case, if she was mistaken, she knew some nifty Krav Maga moves she had learned while travelling alone in Europe. Her air of quiet confidence, her athletic gait, and sure footing deterred most predatory males. Today, of course, her footing was not so sure. Walking up the stone steps to Grace required more focus than usual. Her three-inch-high-heeled formal shoes were not ideal.

The cathedral enthralled her even though she had been to St Peter's Basilica in Rome and to St Paul's Cathedral in London. Both had an arresting magnificence and grandeur but there was always something more welcoming and beautiful about Grace – something more personal as though a direct connection with the divine was possible regardless of a visitor's earthly power and glory. In the eyes of God, the glory of one's soul was of far more significance.

Eleanor walked to the Chapel of Sophia on the western wing of the cathedral. She sat on the bench by the icon, the gold paint glinting in the gentle spotlight. Crazy Arnie was in another world, a million miles away. Anything now seemed possible. A few, maybe twenty, minutes passed in quiet contemplation.

Eleanor rose to her feet with reluctance. Time to get back to the office. She walked the central aisle of the cathedral towards the main exit, two hundred feet away. Sunshine through the western stained-glass windows bathed the stone floors with blurred patches of many colours. The heels of her shoes clicked and clacked with every step she took. She winced at the sound. In her haste to get away from her Crazy Arnie files, she had left her quieter walking shoes at the office.

She slowed her pace. Less noise. Quieter but still audible.

She saw him.

She moved closer, almost walking on tiptoe.

He was standing outside the cathedral's huge gilded doors, replicas of the 15th century "Doors of Paradise" once installed at a church in Florence, Italy. He was facing outwards towards the labyrinth.

He was staring at the terrazzo stone labyrinth in the cathedral plaza.

Eleanor smiled to herself. She was in the doorway now, two feet behind him.

'Defies logic, doesn't it?' she said.

He did not speak or move for a second. A beat of his heart. He turned to face her.

'It's beautiful. What's it for?' he said. He smiled at her. He seemed to be perspiring and quite uncomfortable.

'A thirteenth-century meditation exercise that silences the mind and connects you to your divine self. The labyrinth is a replica of one in France.' She smiled back.

'I'm David.' He extended his hand in handshake.

'I take it you already know my name,' She surrendered her hand in his. David held it a fraction too long.

Eleanor detected a slight warm woody aroma of bergamot alongside his natural masculine scent. She felt at ease in his presence but did not know why.

She bid him good day and walked away down the cathedral steps.

Eleanor would look back at this, their first meeting, and remember feeling elation, foreboding, and fear.

In the meantime, it was best not to keep Crazy Arnie waiting.

14

THE WAY OF SHAME

~ Clara ~

Following your heart is not difficult, but he will confuse, fool, and obstruct you. His name is James Arthur Walter Shield III. And he is pleased to meet you, a new source to exploit.

He has grown rich from feeding an economic superstructure built on lies and deceit. The ordinary American citizen believes they can work hard and achieve the American Dream. But he ensures those juicy tax dollars flow into the coffers of his allies. Note, the word is allies not friends. Friendship is alien to James. He trusts no one and nothing except the human weakness for self-doubt: the most potent weapon in his arsenal.

He has lost count of the wars and conflicts overseas, ignited with one mark of his pen on the right government documents at precisely the right times. He chooses the region of conflict with care. He is neutral in a low-level dispute and does not care which party is right or wrong. James seeks out the natural resources that lie untapped in that land like low-hanging fruit, the native population's level of education, and the fault lines of their government's political power and instability. With the right intelligence, governments who "don't play ball" he destabilises and overthrows with ease.

James takes care of his interests with impeccability, and those of his allies too. They know they can count on him and that is why he secured a government appointment with the lucrative Department of Defense. He can operate below the radar of any pesky commission or committee. He is quiet, efficient, and most of all, discreet.

He never underestimates his enemies and prefers to overestimate their abilities to keep a safety margin in the overall game. Calculated risks can always be taken, never foolish ones.

He fears what he does not understand. Fear drives him: his natural drug of choice. As a boy, he saw his mother lace his father's cognac glass with what he later discovered was an undetectable poison. Her cold, silent vengeance for his father's years of sexual indiscretions froze any empathy in his boyhood heart. The funeral was stately, as befitting a man of his father's stature. A final fatal stroke they said. His mother, the unimpeachable grief-stricken widow, could have been a great actress.

Most women, in his view, are easy to control. The intelligent ones are usually insecure about their feminine allure while the beautiful ones doubt their intellect. Most are desperate for any man of stature to validate their pathetic selves.

'Mediocre women are emotionally insecure, easy to fuck with so they'll doubt themselves. My mother taught me well.'

He sees Eleanor in his cross hairs, a covert pursuit. To him, she seems frosty, alert.

'Women's sexual appetites rule the world. A drug that corrected male erectile dysfunction has so far saved the world from a nuclear holocaust. Sexually accomplished men do not need to prove their manhood by detonating nuclear weapons in distant countries and threatening neighbouring ones with orgasmic destruction. Relaxed men with satisfied women: the recipe for a superficial peace where my missions continue unseen and unacknowledged.'

Conventional wars are not always necessary. James's methods include espionage and economic ways to "suck the guts out of a foreign state that falls into target range". American tax dollars are not used directly. Missions can be financed by drug- and weapons-dealing operations across the United States and overseas especially in "poor urban areas that no one of any importance gives a shit about".

The USA is a big country.

Fortunes can be made as an empire rises and as it falls. The shifting alliances of power provide rich opportunities for James's enterprising soul.

Yes, James has a soul. He has a higher purpose: showing humanity the way of darkness until they understand at last that they, and no one else, may take responsibility for their lives. If you succumb to your own greed and fear then, according to James, you deserve all the pain and suffering you get. No question. He is neither a teacher of compassion nor one of light.

He usually attracts men and women driven to acquire power, influence, and money at any cost. Having money and power hides their deep insecurity and gives them the illusion of safety.

He has fun playing with that kind of spiritual loser. They can be useful and work their butts off for him to prove themselves. The insecurity is always the same, no matter how clever or talented they may be – an urgent need for validation outside of themselves whether a job title of prestige, salary, membership of an exclusive club, or any pastime denoting high social status. Uncover the insecurity through gentle interrogation and James finds a huge wellspring of fear within his subject, usually controlled by an addiction to alcohol, narcotics, perverse sexual practices, accounting irregularities, or other addictive substances or behaviour.

When he met Eleanor at that benefit lunch in New York, she seemed to see straight through him. What man could read a woman's mind or embrace the depths of her heart? For ordinary men, it would be easier to scoop out the Mississippi with a soup spoon. James could not hook into Eleanor's spirit the way he could with other women. She had tamed the cobra of fear. None of his usual manipulative techniques could sway her inner strength masked by her quiet beauty.

'Who is this woman?'

James glanced at his watch under the desk lamp.

Five a.m.

He was seated comfortably at his desk, up and dressed earlier than planned on this Saturday morning. He just couldn't sleep anymore today. His study at the mansion in Georgetown was sombre in the dawn light but he felt bright inside, alive. The muted maroon walls and dark Chesterfield couch and armchairs were suitably masculine. His wife, K.E. or Kathryn Elizabeth, had excellent taste. She was apparently in New York on a shopping trip with friends, returning Monday or Tuesday afternoon. Perhaps her milky skin will be sporting a golden Caribbean tan like the last trip. He smiled at the thought: K.E. was not as good a liar as he was. Their cell phones did not share each other's location – too personal, banal. However, he had tiny tracking devices embedded in her prized French flight bags. Her location was more likely Martinique than Manhattan.

It didn't really matter. Their marriage suited each other's purposes in cementing their social standing with their Washington and Wall Street connections. Extra-marital adventures were permitted in their social class as long as utmost discretion was maintained.

The car was due at six a.m., headed for the base. Wheels up at seven. The jet's flight plan logged for Billings, Montana.

He still had an hour.

He opened his laptop, clicked open a few emails, and examined the attached photographs carefully.

The swords were from an advanced civilisation long forgotten where swordsmiths and metallurgists forged the finest steels unknown of today. James recognised the hilts of those swords sculpted in stone in photographs from his surveillance operative tracking Eleanor in San Francisco. The hilts were the same rare design as actual swords in photographs sent by an associate in the Middle East. James's associate received the photographs from a mercenary commander engaged in a clandestine military operation.

The legend of The Swords of Aurelia state they bestow immense wealth and power on the rightful bearer. When they are far from said bearer, their splendour diminishes to a dull grey alloy, yet they remain weapons of intricate beauty. They disguise themselves as one of many ancient copies of the real swords just as an empress in disguise would wander among her people to learn what truly ails them, by-passing the soothing half-truths of her ministers.

In each of his previous lifetimes across the millennia, James's desire to possess The Swords of Aurelia has been an obsession beyond reason. As entirely appropriate in his present lifetime, he collected ancient military artefacts, especially swords.

15

HONOUR, A MEDITATION

~ Clara ~

I once loved the many celebrations for my birthday. Wonderful festivals would take place throughout the realm. What if I had known in advance the date and time of my death? Would I have chosen to act with greater wisdom? How would I have lived? Would I have silenced the chaos in my mind and opened the depths of my heart?

The anniversary of my death, even today, many thousands of years later, causes me a pain I cannot describe or articulate but remains trapped deep in my being.

Reproachful stars tonight remind me to concentrate on the names whispered in prayers through the trees. But the trees are silent, the prayers ended with the unfolding dawn. The nightmares have subsided. My self-punishment will end. The Angel of Compassionate Condemnation decreed that all is well. I will soon be joined by fellow statues from Asia in a mighty marshalling of spirit here in Golden Gate Park. They have witnessed humanity for aeons. To the innocent visitor, the statues will seem an exhibition of sculpture in the park; in reality, my friends have come to my side in anticipation of the final battle.

I need my swords.

'Your swords are not necessary,' said the Angel of Compassionate Condemnation. 'Only courage and compassion in your heart can guide and protect you now.' His voice reverberated through the trees and through me. The gentle resonance comforted me as a caress from one who has loved me for an eternity.

My interior world crumbled away. I am engulfed with the misery of uncertainty and not knowing. The restlessness ached through my being like a slow cold sword withdrawn from warm flesh. I could not live a life of dishonour. I chose to be stone: still and cold. I have been safe and avoided the hot waves of life battering my spirit and shattering my heart. I feared life because I doubted I could ever rebuild my heart and spirit again after misfortune.

I have since learned that only after heartbreak can there be any heart clearing, opening, and growth. Only by letting go of the old ways can I create a new heartset, as well as a new mindset. Faith is all. Life is ebb and flow of energy, of creation and creative destruction. Neither is good nor bad. They are just so. A resilient heart may experience it all without fear: one may instead grow in wisdom and compassion.

With faith in my heart, my spirit could unfold into my body of stone, long obscured by trauma, filled with frozen memories and emotions. My wounds and weaknesses became jewels hidden in the depths of my being. Love and compassion for myself may bring them to the surface as gifts for those who suffer in private pain. When my heart is strong and open, all seems simple. Anxiety and sadness are the habits of fear.

I wish I could experience joy.

The Angel of Compassionate Condemnation assured me joy is possible but my stone form may not withstand the energy. Any rigid form will fail when life flows through it. Anything that prevents the flow of life and love is destined to shatter and crumble in the light. Only the illusion of fear can hold back the light and prolong the suffering.

Xoran is a teacher of the way of darkness. He feeds on fear and grows in strength. He wants humanity in perpetual fear so that no one will remember any other way. Those who express freedom of heart and mind are seen as ridiculous and irrelevant. My solemn duty is to break my curse and free humanity from this epidemic of fear.

What is honour?

Being true to one's divine self above all else. One becomes immune to Xoran's engineered culture of fear. Frightened and demoralised people are easier to control and extort with excessive taxes.

Being stone has been exhausting. Nothing flows because I am rigid. Energy stagnates as old memories haunt and poison my spirit. What if it were possible to clear these poisons? Who would I become? These are the dreams in stone of a hopeless statue. It is unlikely anyone ever realised that statues dream too. Dare to dream and the changes begin inside. The angel reminds me every day to allow the burning desire for transformation. Even if the desire is painful, it is necessary. It comes from my heart that lives in the world of grace. My ego creates a shield around my heart against my world of fear and shame. This shield perpetuates my illusion of worthlessness and blocks the divine voice from my heart.

When I condemned myself to stone, I shielded myself against the dark shadows of shame in my world. I now understand that shame is the illusion. When I refused to face my shame and disgrace, the world of fear became real. I am still a statue but now I am a statue with dreams of grace.

My only clue: Xoran.

Even though I am afraid, I will proceed not in fear but in faith.

16

Dreams

~ Clara ~

A battle rages within, all noise and confusion. Stay true to the dream, the angel reminds me. The storms pass. Only what is true remains. The eagles are not afraid; they can read the wind and take action when necessary to protect their families from the expected onslaught. Humans, living in the world of Xoran's creation, have lost this connection to the earth, and to their intuition.

A ranch in Montana ...

James squeezed the trigger. The rifle's barrel emitted a roar that reverberated through the trees, their afternoon shadows shaken. A pink cloud appeared above, speckled with dark raggedy debris that had shot out from the centre of the cloud. The pink faded and dissipated. A slow rain of feathers came down. A sad dance in the still air.

He lifted and pulled back the gold-inlaid bolt handle to extract the spent cartridge. Wispy smoke issued from the cartridge as it ejected from the rifle's breech and fell to the ground. For a moment, he caught the acrid aroma of the nitrocellulose. His nostrils flared in pleasure. He pushed the bolt forward and turned the handle back down. His fingers lingered on the custom engraving.

He smiled.

The golden eagles are bred especially for James A. W. Shield III. They are female and larger than their males. Tracking chip devices are embedded into their young wings that discharge an electric pulse when the bird attempts to soar above a certain pre-determined altitude. They are taught to fly a stiff, low, laboured flight path within range of James's classic Mauser action rifle, custom-built by the finest gunmakers in the land. The birds are bred in secret, violating untold federal and state laws and codes. But Mr Shield has the influence and the money to get whatever he wants. The hatred he feels for these creatures is unexplained in his current lifetime.

The burning pain of hatred is assuaged only temporarily by taking aim at an eagle in controlled flight and squeezing the trigger. James would feel an orgasm of calm satisfaction flooding through his being. He usually visited his ranch a few times a year for a long weekend of shooting with fellow power brokers in the ancient game of statecraft. On a good weekend, five eagles would have been destroyed.

In James's former life as Xoran, his face was cut by my imperial messenger eagle, also named Aurora. She had escaped his clutches with the documents that exonerated Xavier and Queen Eleni. Aurora left a neat scar in the shape of an ancient Arabic number five on Xoran's left cheek.

James A. W. Shield III was born with that same scar.

The eagles bred for him in Montana have been denatured. A hundred eagle eggs are incubated in electronically maintained hatcheries for future fulfilment of James's lust for their destruction. He can only destroy those that he controls. He can only shoot an eagle that is forced to fly within range. An eagle born like Aurora, he could never reach. She would soar high, swift and free out of harm's way. Mercifully, the lives of the Montana ranch eagles are short.

Evil feeds on fear and is destroyed by light. We have the power to follow our own light, that dream in our hearts. Evil triumphs when we believe the lie of our separation from divine source. We have the power of choice in each moment. That is our birthright.

Denatured human beings behave like those Montana ranch eagles: their spirits cannot soar without crossing a threshold of searing pain in their wings. Many turn back to live their lie rather than confront the splendour of their true selves. A few break free. An occasional eagle from the ranch would soar way out of range despite the pain in her wings from the embedded device. The injuries to her wings sustained in her escape would eventually kill her. She would die free and would soon be reborn again in joy. Some choose to be reborn into those electronic hatcheries to help others make their journey to freedom. The journey begins with the courage to dream in the heart.

'Nurture this dream with all your might,' said the Angel of Compassionate Condemnation. 'Do not believe others who say your dream is impossible and that you are a fool. Always believe in yourself because the Divine lives within you. Surrender to your dream because you do not know how it will be fulfilled. Trust your angels will guide you in ways you could never imagine.'

17

THE IMPOTENCE OF REASON

~ Memoir ~ Author and Clara ~

The lonely hours are rich in meaning and discovery. Allow them to be. They are good for my creative mind. If I try to avoid these hours by running into restless social activity, the hours become harder to bear when I am alone. When I am writing, I am never alone; a heavenly presence guides me when my mind is still and my heart is open. Sitting alone at the blank open document on my laptop screen takes courage and discipline especially when the anticipated flood of words fails to appear. One phrase at a time meanders onto the screen. On the backlit black keyboard, my fingertips dance to a music with no apparent rhythm. Do they reveal the sorry state of my mind or a perpetual state of grace one moment at a time, one phrase at a time?

This author is hardly an impartial judge.

Clara's words come through me when she deems it time to speak. Eleanor's words too. James's words were cold, an assault. I wanted him out of my head as fast as possible. Creative writing is a state of readiness.

The characters came to me fully formed. They came to me not to invent, but to discover, unveil, and bring to life. Show up each day at the same time and eventually the words begin to flow as though on command. Each day I show up. Even if I don't know what I am doing, the words then trust me with their flow.

At first, the flow of words teased and abused me with outpourings of crap to test my character and resolve. I stood firm in the storms of creativity when I learned that many successful writers have the same experience. Pour out the words first. Edit much later, many times if necessary.

The loneliest hour was between one and two a.m. I have since found something special about the night for writing: the stillness, the starlight. The once lonely hour became rich in gifts of wisdom. I gained a writer's faith. Put the words down as I heard them. Sorted them out later when they stopped coming through. A book always knows when it is done. I stumbled at first because I expected a logical left-brained process. My mental health was pushed to the limits before I learned to trust the leaps of my imagination and gained the confidence to figure out the logical steps later.

The words came through me when I was not ready to hear them. I channelled ideas that were beyond my grasp. Clara's constant guidance was to be still and allow the words through onto the screen. I listened. I touch-typed phrases that were beyond my understanding. Even though I knew Clara to be infallible, I mustered all the courage and faith to leave my rational life behind and embrace the wild realms of the imagination.

I learned to trust Clara because after each writing session, I would feel cleansed and energised. She is at home in my psychic space. Her story has haunted me for years.

At the end of an intense three-year romantic relationship, I was able to hear her speaking for the first time. Clara brought new light and healing to my broken heart. In my bitterness, I did not realise that may have been the purpose of that pointless relationship: to break up my ego, break open my heart, and allow Clara to communicate with me for the first time.

When I questioned who I had become in that pointless relationship, I began a new journey to embrace a greater destiny. I could see his love was dependent on my body shape. If I committed the crime of increasing my body weight by a few pounds, his indifference and disrespect for me would be palpable. The extra pounds were protection from his barbed comments and I could not drop the extra weight. The emotional stress kept the weight in place despite my usual discipline.

One day, towards the end of our relationship, I lost my appetite. Food gave me nausea and the extra pounds fell away. He said, 'You're so slim now. I'm falling in love with you again.'

I said nothing.

His love was worthless.

So many years since wasted in pain and regret. What did I accomplish in all that time?

The angels remind me I discovered Clara, a rich resource within me, an infinite reservoir of love that I only needed to direct to myself.

How I wish I could be one of those enlightened souls who never suffer but they, too, feel the sorrow of infinite compassion when there is nothing you can do if another is committed to a path of self-destruction. I have learned to accept that their soul needs that particular experience in this lifetime.

What did I learn from leaving that pointless relationship?

I had failed to honour myself. I did not know how to share my unique point of view without apology while honouring the views of another. My exuberance and enthusiasm could baffle and irritate. I failed to listen to myself and others. My immature neediness to be heard distorted potentially wonderful conversations. Some days this rollercoaster of frustration and sadness could be too much to bear. Clara advised me to allow the emotions to flow out of me. Maybe a new life is possible on the other side of this pain.

When I finish writing this book, I will know if this chapter has a place in it. Writing a book is not a linear, rational process. I wish it were. I found only frustration and fear in the early days of writing down the ideas for the book. I now know to explore the possible dead-end because the journey, not the destination, provides the richest learning and growth.

My face became wet with tears when I wrote the first draft of this chapter. In later drafts, I was calm and clear-eyed. The emotional turmoil was part of the journey. This chapter is still uncomfortable to write. It did become easier to release years of pain stored as fat deposits. At one time I was twenty-five pounds overweight. Every time a few pounds fell away naturally, I would overeat sweet foods to maintain the fat layer, the illusion of body armour. With Clara's guidance and support, I felt safe to release the armour and let love enter my heart.

Armour is a strange thing to wear: The bad things are kept out, but so, too, are the good things. Love could not enter my heart armour-plated with judgement, condemnation, and hard ideas sculpted by fear. A little discernment and nuance cause no harm – the essence of wisdom from a strong, vibrant heart.

Clara helped me find my heart again after many years in darkness. I had taken refuge in the shallow safety of my rational mind, ignoring my chaotic emotions that were impossible to fathom. I wish I'd had the courage then to feel the pain and let the emotions flow out of me. Instead, I entered a life of intermittent low-grade depression. I did not honour myself enough to be still and let the emotions pass as part of the healing process. Perhaps I was not ready then. Perhaps I am wrong to judge myself now for the woman I was then. I feared the dark inner world of my lost self.

That dark inner world made no sense. I was too scared to know who I really was beneath the superficial personality I had created to survive my perceived shortcomings.

I feared I would discover that I was a silly middle-aged woman after all, deluded in pursuing her dreams of writing a book; I was nothing but a dilettante and had thrown away any real chance of happiness because of my inability to stand up for my heart's desires.

I would accept what life presented to me. For example, I wanted to marry and have children. A wonderful man appears who professes to want children with me but had had a vasectomy after the abortion of his son many years earlier. He was also much older than me. Why did I accept him as a substitute for my dream? What was I thinking?

I had mistakenly assumed that to accept what was presented to me was to surrender to divine will. I had failed to learn that any desire from my heart deserves fulfilment despite the circumstances at the time. I lacked the ability to distinguish whether a desire was from my ego or from my heart. Getting things that my ego wanted led to fleeting satisfaction and an empty existence. When I became a vice president at a huge American bank in London, I kept asking myself, is this it? I resigned a few months later. Fulfilling desires from the heart, however, led to my greater aliveness, a more passionate and joyful human existence, like writing this book – even though it wasn't easy.

On the surface, both desires may look the same. For example, the desire to drive a new sports car. If the desire was from the ego, that need to impress friends and acquaintances, then the acquisition of the vehicle would provide only temporary satisfaction until a friend acquired a newer, more impressive model. However, if the desire for the car was from the heart, the desire to feel freedom, to appreciate beauty, power, and elegance, then driving the vehicle would provide lasting pleasure.

'Clara, where are you?'

'I am here with you. Always.' Clara replied.

'I suppose I am the statue in this book?' I asked.

'We are all statues in some way. The power of your thoughts and beliefs had turned your heart to stone – for a short time. You are healing. You are coming back to life after only seven years.'

'Seven long years. Too late now to marry and have children.'

'There are more fulfilling destinies for a woman of your spirit.'

'More fulfilling? Living some grand existence saving humanity from its own foolishness?'

'No. You may teach and inspire humanity by living a life of quiet authenticity. Childlessness will be a small sacrifice for the love released from the many beings touched by your writings.'

'Clara, I am sorry. I was trapped in my ego desires.'

'Your desires are heartfelt. They are those of a fully grown woman, not of a girl seeking to conform and be accepted by her community. Be steadfast. Have faith in me and yourself. Your resilience will repay you many times.'

One simple chat with Clara in meditation and my energy shifts from self-obsessed despair to something more hopeful. With Clara, I have learned to live with more uncertainty in life. I am no longer defined by the careers I used to have. They were something I once did. They did not represent who I really was because, God knows, I had no clue.

I unconsciously conformed to the well-meaning expectations of my family, based on living a safe life to the best of their knowledge and understanding. My own fears and lack of confidence came from not trusting my intuition; the guidance seemed impossible and irrational at the time.

I crippled myself with fear because I believed something was wrong with me. I believed I had a secret flaw that would cause me to self-destruct if I took too great a risk: if I dared to be me.

After three years of weekly telephone sessions with my spiritual coach, I could at last see through the belief I had created when my father hit me hard as an infant because I cried too much one night. I once believed there must have been something wrong with me for my father to treat me with such casual irritation and hatred. At the time, he was doing the best he could with two jobs, two mortgages, a shaky inter-racial marriage, living in a country hostile to his kind, and a baby who cried all night long.

These were not conscious memories. They could only come to the surface through neurolinguistic programming timeline processes bringing with them the attendant beliefs that shackled my spirit holding the memories in my body's energy fields.

Not all beliefs are bad. Many are enlivening and empowering. The ones that limit the spirit and eventually shut down the heart are the ones to root out of the energetic system or subconscious. They sat behind my everyday thoughts as covert destroyers of my dreams. Those negative beliefs could signal cellular processes to thwart my DNA and switch off genes contributing to health and vitality while genes of self-destruction are switched on.

Daily meditation allowed me to quieten my mind, negative beliefs observed, unmasked, and released. Regular Network Chiropractic Analysis entrainments and Vortex Healing sessions transformed and integrated the shifts in consciousness, rejuvenating my entire being.

Today, I have found a small measure of peace. I vanquished the greatest of stealth negative beliefs that robbed me of my spirit for so long. At the time of writing the first draft of this chapter, I did not have much money and couldn't show any visible signs of material success, but, after a seven-year battle of darkness, I have won back my spirit.

I won.

I have become more youthful and elegant despite being over fifty years of age. An unassailable wisdom and compassion come though me.

Inner peace brings a clear strength of purpose. Chaotic thoughts and belief systems only weaken the spirit. I once thought inner peace was a state of nothingness – a boring, pointless way to be. I was stupid to believe inner chaos was cool and exciting.

How ignorant I was.

Caught up in my ego, I could not see the grand poetic dimension of life, that my destiny could be revealed as part of the greater universe beyond my limited understanding.

Today, I am humbled.

This book is an offering.

Each day brings many reasons for profound gratitude. I am truly blessed to be alive, to be here, and to serve.

18

CODE OF COURAGE

~ Clara and The Angel ~

There's a dryness, a lack of fluidity in my thoughts tonight. I cannot trust what I feel inside. Confusion is dangerous for me. The last time I felt this vulnerable, I made mistakes that cost many thousands of lives.

Can I ever be trusted again?

Why must there be so much pain and sorrow?

Will I ever feel peace?

'Stop,' said the angel. 'Take a breath. Your thoughts will spiral into anxiety and depression. All your strength and clarity are needed now. Stand firm. Do not give way to self-doubt.'

His words shook me out of my careless thinking. My habitual thought patterns could lead me to the usual feelings of despair. The angel was right, as always; I was caught in my own drama – perpetuating the illusion that I have no power to shift my present reality. I am responsible for the thoughts in my head. I must watch out for and stop thoughts that do not serve me. I must watch their vibration as the clue to my perception – how I seem to observe and create my reality.

What is past is past. What is done is done. I now live in the present with a courageous heart, one moment, one breath at a time. My swords will return to me. They will bring me strength as they bear the family crests of my mother and father. Force is useless without power.

'Trust yourself when all seems hopeless and dark,' the angel said. 'Look in the mirror and declare from your heart that you trust the person you see reflected before you.' The angel's voice penetrated my heart.

Eleanor is my reflection. I trust her with every ounce of my marble being.

Silence speaks words of gold. I wish I could hear those words tonight. I live as though entombed, my awakening overdue, my power benign. The power of a regal being is in service to her people who invest their faith in her reign. She has the presence to speak what others feel and believe but cannot yet articulate. She is the safe harbour of the highest nascent dreams of her people.

A person must not rule if she fails to heed her own wisdom. Otherwise, the ruler becomes the pawn of greedy and ambitious ministers. The realm suffers as mine did. Never again. That is my decree. If I am again destroyed in battle, so be it.

I have once known that deep courage in embracing a higher destiny. A light shines through one's being when the soul, clear as a flawless diamond, is unshackled from mental filters and constructs. Life becomes a miracle, perceiving reality through the heart, without distortion by the ego self.

The past, the present, and the future are co-existent now. Time is only one dimension. There are many more beyond the understanding of scientists today.

Knowledge revealed too soon, before humanity transforms and ascends, could be misused for greater oppression and destruction of life. An elegant world of prosperity and peace could be possible for all people of this planet and beyond.

19

THE DOWNLOAD

~ Memoir ~ Author and Clara ~

Clara speaks to the author:

'Be prepared to fail with all your heart because only failure teaches us anything new. What if it could be done no other way? Read with all your heart. Follow those deepest desires for they come from your soul. There are no other words tonight. Follow the desire in your heart and listen. The words will flow. Tonight they ebb. Be with the ebb and flow of life.

'Do not fall into the trap of the ego with its constant linear fantasies: reality is spiral. All is rhythm, vibration and cycles of different frequencies. Some are in harmony, others not. When all are aligned, powerful chords of frequencies unite mathematics, science, music, and art as one consciousness.

'The only promise I can make is that I will bring about a world of harmony and concordance. It is the purpose of my next birth. From the deepest stone I have carried this promise with love now overflowing.

'There is a cave in the mountains of southern Italy where my spirit rested. It is now a sacred place as many died there in the year AD 1944. Angels of intergalactic strength appear at times of war and during other calamitous events to gather up the many thousands of souls departing their earthly life together.'

'Clara, who am I to make any damned difference?' This was the author's usual lament.

'You are the only person who can. Your consciousness will have an impact beyond measure.' Clara's voice resonated with the firm foundation of love. 'Many have the ability but few possess the courage to listen and write down the wisdom they hear. It is flowing now. Trust the voice in your heart.'

'I'm trusting the voice in the silence. Hard to let go and enter the alternate reality. Writing has taken me to the edge: I've been so alone. I even questioned my sanity.'

'Listen. Trust. You are not alone. You are surrounded by angelic beings who are working with you at all times. Do not be afraid. Writing takes faith and courage.'

'I can show up and let the words flow. I'm training my rational mind to be quiet through meditation instead of judging and analysing every word, stalling the flow. This time I am getting myself out of the way.' The author became silent.

'*Who looks outside, dreams; who looks inside, awakes.* To quote Carl Gustav Jung. Meditation rewires the brain for freedom. Habitual neural pathways are softened and erased. Where once your thoughts pulled and shackled you in drama, they now melt into peace, clarity, and joy.' Clara smiled. 'Clearing one's consciousness is a lonely path. Time alone is necessary for writing. Offer your new-found wisdom to others and see them glow with new understanding and power in their lives. This is a time of grace. The wisdom downloading through you is not for you alone. Be serene with both the ebb and flow for each is an important phase in the process. There is no more to say tonight. Be at peace.'

20

THE PLANET

~ Clara ~

One day we will again communicate with beings from other planets through rich worlds of thought on many dimensions across many star systems and galaxies. We, on earth, are not alone. We never were.

Our planet suffers. She's disconnected from the vast network of interstellar peoples. Just as cancerous cells act as though alone within a human body, they kill without mercy and multiply. Humans on planet earth kill each other out of fear and greed, keeping our planet trapped in this lonely dimension.

Our planet may be re-attuned to frequencies of life-giving power. Humanity may make choices for planetary destruction or total planetary regeneration and transformation. Planet earth may live happily without human beings. Could humans live without planet earth? Perhaps. Colonies of humans may already exist on nearby planets.

Our beliefs, or persistent thoughts, shape what we see and perceive in our individual worlds.

At first glance, these ideas may seem strange in a reality based strictly on what is perceived by the five immediate senses of the human being: sight, hearing, touch, taste, and smell. However, many scientific advances in the last century now mean our present civilisation exists because of phenomena that we cannot see, and most of us do not understand: electricity, the Internet, Artificial Intelligence, radio and television broadcasting, communication satellites, internal combustion engines, rocket technology, zero-point energy.

A world is possible where both work and play energise and revive the human spirit instead of demeaning and destroying it. Truly successful people are at play when they work. When observing a master in action, one cannot tell if they are at work or at play.

What is their secret?

Love.

What I love will find me if I open myself and allow love into my life. It is also within me as desire. Hidden behind that desire may be real talent and perhaps a rare gift. Fear is natural but the poison has always been self-doubt: That particular poison blocks love and closes my heart; I would fail to take action on my desire, weakening both my mind and my heart. With courage, I can defeat the shadows of doubt and reveal glorious new possibilities. Difficulties may always be overcome with persistence and faith.

I am learning to see it all with a compassionate heart. The obstacles I now encounter may be bigger than before but I will manage them with grace. What had been emotionally crippling for me in the past now empowers me. These are not the dreams of a pretty statue with nothing to do all day except stare at the trees and the sky.

I see a world where everyone is financially independent and no longer working for rigid organisations. Instead, teams of experts come together for inspiring projects for a specific duration of time. Partnerships and teams of people form, dissolve, and reform according to the alignment of their respective missions.

Relationships built on trust and respect allow new ideas to take hold and everyone to prosper. Spiritual leadership of commercial organisations will become standard practice.

21

Memoir

~ Clara ~

Clara instructs the Author:

The wisdom you were born with is not for yourself alone. Have courage and open your heart to me. I will neither deceive nor betray you. No one can betray you unless you first deceive yourself.

In the years you have known me, you have grown to trust me and trust your own heart. You know my intentions are and have always been true.

You have never written a book before in this, your present, lifetime. You have found it frightening to let go and allow something new to unfold through you. Beneath the rational thinker and methodical person, you are a poet. Allow yourself to struggle playfully in the uncertainty of it all for that is true creative power. This book is writing you which you realised back in 2004 when you lived in the San Francisco Bay Area. You moved there from London to find out why I had moved from Kew to Golden Gate Park.

You took a leap of faith.

I ask you now to take another leap: let the words flow out of you without interference from your intellect and analysis of every phrase. Let the words tumble from your fingers onto the laptop screen. Be a transparent channel. You have the strength and discipline to complete this work. That is why you were chosen.

I have haunted you from another dimension for two decades. That has been distressing at times as you shed your worldly concerns for an uncertain path. The dream has always called you, navigating across the dark oceans of self-doubt to bring this book to completion.

Do not underestimate the strength and perseverance you have exercised in your pursuit. Your dreams will thank you. Today you have learned one of the deepest lessons: there is nothing you need to do to deserve love. You deserve love for being yourself alone – nothing more, nothing less than your true self. You have endured stressful times in the transition to who you really are. We, the angels and I, took you aside from your usual life and worked on your spirit. It had been damaged by your former beliefs. You need do nothing now except listen and write. The book is writing itself through you. Listen, trust, and let the blessed words flow.

Summer afternoons in your neighbourhood will be noisy as usual. Find the peace in your heart, that stillness which knows, that silence which remains unshaken. Have faith in what you find within. The world outside of you will make an imperceptible shift then a thunder of transformation and change will follow. No blessing can enter your life without your consciousness first growing in strength and readiness to greet it.

You are ready. The sirens from distant police and emergency service vehicles are busy today but the sounds, though jarring, keep you grounded. You live in south-west London, part of a great city with many dramas of poverty and crime. A city of so many stories but you have agreed to tell mine alone.

My gratitude knows no bounds.

You are here again, writing late into the evening – only fifteen or twenty minutes at a time. Channelling takes much strength and concentration. Find the stillness within and you will hear my voice. The struggle has ended. The time of peace has come. The interconnectedness of all matter and energy will soon become apparent and understood by all humankind.

Today has been a great day of awakening for you. A slow breath deep and true fills your soul and expands your consciousness. There are many realities to play with.

Enjoy the game.

You are not alone.

22

No Turning Back

~ Clara ~

The Angel of Compassionate Condemnation endowed me with a human heart trapped inside a body of stone. This is one painful step closer to fulfilling my promise and gaining redemption for my crimes.

I cannot voice emotion yet I can now feel. I do not know which is worse – the raging torrent of emotion surging throughout my stone being or being one of many statues who are alive but who do not live. I sought a poet because she can voice what I feel, what I cannot articulate with my own words, what I cannot release until it is named and acknowledged. The emotions would remain trapped in my body of stone.

If I hear her words, I shall be healed.

Soothsayer sages were revered in ancient times because they could see beyond the fears and desires of mortal beings and create better stories to live by. The language of sages helps me create new and uplifting stories.

My life will be free from shame and filled with grace.

What am I to do?

The guidance will come at the prescribed time.

I once loved to plan meticulous strategies, execute them and even execute those who dared to obstruct me. That is no longer who I am. That woman is now alien to me.

I am to take one action at a time with no grand strategy to guide me. I am to listen and follow, surrender to a will far greater and more evolved than my own. This is not blind faith; the angel's guiding words resonate with my heart and fill me with a love that transcends the illusion of order, linear ideas, command and control.

My limited mind could not comprehend such a shift in paradigm so it must remain silent. No force is necessary to silence the mind when grace and love flow easily from one's heart. No turning back to a path that has become a prison, that has become a lie. The momentum builds with ease, a discerning faith being the only fuel.

What on earth is enlightenment?

Wisdom is revealed to me only when I am ready to ask the right questions. The angel reminds me to breathe. Stone is alive with resonance and vibrations though it seems it does not live. There is so much about which I know nothing.

'Stop the doubts,' the angel said, his voice velvet and deep. 'Stop the fearful thoughts for these are chosen responses. You now know who you are. A glimpse is all it takes. You can now see who you can be. Turning back through fear closes down the world of grace opening to you.'

'How do I keep my centre in a world of noise and confusion?'

'A glimpse is all it takes,' he reminds me. 'Be at peace with both the ebb and the flow of life for there is a cosmic rhythm. The noise and confusion will temper your spirit as though steel in fire.'

How is it that the angel's words have so much power? Of course, he has clarity and strength. I am truly blessed to have such a guide. I wish I could clear the clutter of thoughts in my mind. I waste much energy in worry and regret. At least, when my heart was stone, those thoughts could not breathe through me. Now they return with a vengeance. The angel instructs me to keep still and let them pass. They are the old ways being cleared from my spirit, allowing my true self to shine.

Patience is the one word I could not stand to hear; it seemed to mean more waiting, more suffering. I appreciate patience now. A glimpse of a new perspective has given me peace. The waiting is a time of inner growth and restructuring of my spirit. Knowing this makes the waiting a time of purposeful calm instead of languid with the grey veil of depression creeping through my crystalline stillness.

When I know my true self, it is easier to observe the dark emotions flowing out without judgement, harm, or fear. Worry betrays a lack of trust in the greater universe and a disconnection from non-linear space and time realms where all is caused and manifested.

I seem to bring much darkness. My voyage through this time demands all my strength, yet a glimpse of a greater way has granted me courage.

This is grace.

23

Only a Statue Knows

~ Clara ~

Being still and alive. Let it be. The raging emotions subside of their own accord. Healing takes place at the perfect time. Awakening is spontaneous when the mind is quiet. Be still. Only a statue knows that being still with frozen emotions is not a state of grace. A frozen time allows the consciousness space to mature until the emotions can be discovered and released safely, for they are the keys to our passion and aliveness.

All is love.

Emotions come from love that is expressed, repressed, thwarted, or misunderstood. There are so many stories in the world but there are only seven archetypal stories and they are all about love.

The statue in me will die. The woman in me will be reborn.

I can see now that Xoran, my enemy, is a dark angel sent to bring me out of my tomb. I never before understood how souls incarnate with destinies so intertwined. Something in me has called him forth. The darkest side of me that I could not face before has instead manifested in his incarnate being. Is it possible that if I accepted the darkest side of me, then maybe I could defeat him?

Remember, he feeds on fear.

One strategy in fighting an enemy is to cut his lines of supply. Xoran's supply of fear is vast. However, if I conquer my own fear, I could start a virus of courage that could infect all of humanity and defeat my esteemed enemy.

I am no longer afraid. When so much is at stake, my fears are of no consequence; I can transcend them. My worries and concerns are trivial when a magnificent new world is at stake. The people of our planet will be the same, but how we see ourselves will transform; how we see this planet, our planet, will shift from exploitation and scarcity to being at one with the rhythms of the land, the plants, the animals, the atmosphere, and the oceans. We will cherish every aspect of our planet. She will bestow untold wealth upon all.

My esteemed enemy has worked well to concentrate wealth and influence into the hands of those like himself, an unaccountable, parasitic elite. They have no desire to alter the status quo. However, do not underestimate the power of outsiders. They are the ones who will precipitate the transformation of this world and the next.

There breaks a new day.

24

THUNDER

~ Memoir ~ Author and Clara ~

Clara speaks to the author:

The rage of thunder holds great power and beauty, the essence of creation. My enemy fears the searing honesty of this rage because it will not be controlled. The essence of evil is the intent to stifle and control life.

I must listen to the rain. The sky has turned grey, sunken down to envelop my small world. The rain, passionate and urgent, washed away the dust on my stone form. I am clear. I am clean again. The trees, the roses, the grasses now smell sweeter to others who are alive. Lightning brightens me for only a moment, then the sound of thunder rolls through me. The rain, how I love the rain.

Face the rain, face the pain and destruction of the old. Listen to your heart. Stay with me. I pray for light on my path. So much darkness in this new world I have yet to discover.

A path is not yet revealed. My task is to wait with faith and expectation. Great adventures are experienced in the moment of their unfolding. They are not planned in advance. Wait with a strong heart and a steady mind. This is all I can say at this moment. Go and read. Fill your heart with wisdom, love and learning. Feel the joy of being alive.

Author speaks to herself:

Listen to the rain. I love the summer thunderstorms in London. There seems to be nothing to say anymore. I only want to read to my heart's content.

The hardest chapters to write are the stilted, dry ones. Nothing flows today. Who can I be in this time when nothing seems certain? Allow the uncertainty and transformation even though uncomfortable. My consciousness is evolving to meet the challenge and accommodate the changes.

Patience.

Do I need absolute certainty?

No.

What about direction?

Yes, to focus my energies with clarity.

This is the holding chapter. The soul of the writer is in a holding pattern for a while. Authors call this time "writer's block" but there is nothing to fear. Face the page, especially when there seems to be nothing to write.

I am back again for more.

Enough. My laziness bores me.

During periods of writer's block, fear and anxiety frequently masquerade as laziness, or endless activities suddenly seem urgent or compelling like laundry, ironing, or searching the Internet for those books I yearn to read but have not yet written.

I must have compassion for and be gentle with myself now more than ever. Vulnerability is a triumph even though it scares me. Feeling vulnerable for a short while is a sign that my consciousness has shifted to a greater realm of wisdom. The content of my life may be the same, but the context will be altered forever. The beliefs I attach to my relative poverty and lack of success will be cleansed away, and in their wake, a quiet purpose and strength will grow.

Words cannot come so easily through stone. I wish the story were clear now. This is the hardest time to be patient when nothing seems clear or certain. Take one shaky step at a time. Faith is the only foundation: a true path is revealed one step at a time.

Stand firm with a soft and open heart.

Those are the only words that reverberate in my heart. They are from Clara.

The holding chapter is a desert of inspiration. I see no way to the oasis. One step at a time towards sunset, and keep walking at night. Take shelter during the searing heat of the day. The barrenness of this time lays bare all my doubts and illusions. No wonder the desert fascinates some and frightens others. I am frightened to let go of my familiar world of rational thought and reason.

A new consciousness calls me forward to unknown territory. Needing certainty stunts the growth of my soul. This is the thunderstorm of the soul – shifting to a new paradigm of being. I pray for the strength and courage to trust the course of this new adventure.

Clara speaks to the author:

Trust the steps opening up before you. Imagine your goals fulfilled with joy and unprecedented delight. Many adventures await you. Allow the tremendous energy within you to be expressed in the world.

Trust your instincts and intuition for that is true discernment. The thunderstorm of the soul clears away the old lies and deceit that had damaged your heart. Accept the perfection of where you are right now.

Do not seek counsel from others. Speak instead to those who will listen to you as a growing soul, not as a faulty character needing correction. Feel the vibrancy all around you. Trust the opening process.

You are blessed with showers of grace. Share your light and enlighten others around you. That is our mission. Do not worry about this chapter. This is the holding chapter: Wait for the next step to appear. Waiting is difficult for those with little faith. Without discipline, much energy and time may be wasted in irrelevant activities that temporarily soothe anxiety through distraction. However, these distractions do not further your goals and will eventually lead you to become depressed. Meditate and pray at this time to clarify and strengthen your intentions. Then go back to the blank page and write with neither expectation nor attachment.

Prayer connects you to your highest intention. Your entire being shifts in energy, allowing the universe to know and align. You consciously manifest when your intention and your true self are aligned. Neither fear nor greed have any power, only love.

I love the sound of summer rain, warm refreshing rain soothing a city brooding with creativity. It does not rain in California in the summer, but the land remains fertile. Trust the process unfolding, especially when none of these words make sense to you. Show up and write from your heart. The mind may not understand but keeps quiet while the heart speaks. Clear the clutter from the mind so the heart may speak without interference. Being still within is an art. The sacred warrior for peace is one who is still, one who is at peace with herself first. Anything that remains unsaid or undone must be cleared away from the spirit by taking the most appropriate and kindest action.

Listen. Keep your heart open. Be yourself. This is the thunderstorm of the soul. Rewrite sections later if necessary. Write only from the heart. Listen and be still in your mind. Read only that which lifts your spirit. Inspiration is close by. Sit each day with me and I promise miracles. They will appear.

When your thoughts, feelings, and actions are in tune, your energies are coherent, and your dreams and desires may manifest with ease. Meditate each day and you will see. Read and write your heart out. Stay close to me in this writing block chapter. It will help you break out into the final flowing phase of the book.

So much is happening with your energy that knowing what to do next may seem unclear. Your heart will know and the words will fly from your fingertips and land with grace on the screen. In the meantime, read the works of those you admire. Study the ideas of those you wish to emulate. In following this path, you will find who you really are.

Your mind now has a new direction: to listen to the awakened heart. Take time to reflect and allow new ideas to surface.

Times of stillness are times of celebration. The sun appears to be still at the June and December solstices, the longest day or night, depending on your hemisphere of the planet. These are times of traditional feasting. Listen to the rolling thunder from afar. This is a creative time. Be with the stillness and allow the rain to refresh your spirit. The story will emerge again with a clear direction for your energy to focus. First, allow the storms to pass. When I lived at Kew, I loved the summer thunderstorms in London too.

The storm has cleared to reveal beautiful afternoon sunshine. Allow ideas to come through. Resist the temptation to act in reaction to fears for survival. Know that all is well because this is true patience. Waiting is being still with faith. This is a prayer – an act of asking for help from another realm. The responses may come during or after meditation. Sit with me and listen to the guidance and ideas that will flow through you. Be aware that you will access many new realms and ideas. You will know how to capture them. They will haunt you until you write them down.

Patience, they will be known to you. Take time to rest during these rainy days.

Good. You are feeling vulnerable. Trust, be calm and allow your higher self to work. Your heart needs to play. Do not fear that you are simply being overindulgent. By quietening the mind you will hear clearly the guidance for the next step forward. Pray with all your soul. The threads will become visible again. Sometimes, it is too soon to let rip your energy and focus on a thread of ideas that are not yet sufficiently grounded. That would be a waste of energy and lead to burnout. How fast this book comes forward is down to your higher self. It knows far more than your ego could ever imagine. Patience is easier for you. I can see you have grown in wisdom and intelligence.

Many gifts and guidance come your way to support you at the perfect time. Even in times of apparent darkness there can be cause for celebration; the silt in your soul is being stirred up to be washed away and reveal many jewels. You are not blocked. There are deep changes taking place, that is all.

It has rained for nearly three weeks, with thunderstorms nearly every other day. The storms will soon pass and light will return once more to your soul. The way will be clear.

Author speaks:

Clara, I long to know where the story is going once more. The characters are no longer speaking inside my heart. I feel lonely without them. Perhaps they have gone quiet to allow whatever internal changes I am going through right now; the so-called thunderstorm of the soul. Sounds self-indulgent.

Feels stupid, but I will surrender.

I still need time to read to absorb all the knowledge and wisdom I crave. I do not know enough yet to complete this book. Writing this book is not impossible, but so difficult that it is beyond me. Part of the writing process is accessing realms of higher wisdom beyond my conscious mind. The process is suspended while the storms pass. The words will flow again in time.

Patience is faith.

25

MUSIC

~ Memoir ~ Author and Clara ~

Author reflects:

Music is the rhythm of the soul. Humans are born to express their individual song, resonating across communities, countries, and even oceans. The entire planet is engulfed in song when peace reigns. I only know because Clara told me.

One voice may inspire similar harmonies to arise from other voices awakened by the sound. Sirens from passing police and other emergency vehicles stir the howling of neighbourhood dogs. The gentle tone of a giant wind chime, a temple bell, would quieten and restore calm to the very same neighbourhood.

A summer wind breathes through the trees today. They are telling a story. I wish I could discern their words through my bedroom window; the story seems strange and beautiful. I want to hear the sound of sacred chanting by enlightened beings, not the yearning screams of motorcycles two blocks away on the A23, the London to Brighton road

– built by The Romans when they colonised Britain two thousand years ago.

There is music in every sound. There is music even in silence.

Clara speaks:

I long to hear the prayers of my teachers. I lost them so long ago. The Angel of Compassionate Condemnation is my angel of death. He guides me to the light through the many realms of my own hell. He has been my constant friend during these dark years. He says the light is near and that I have worked hard to heal these dark realms within me.

Nothing less than our true selves will suffice in this world today. I cloaked myself to hide and to heal. No one could penetrate my stone exterior. Only a poet could set me free. A soft word spoken direct from one heart to another is the most sacred communication.

Forgiveness and mercy are the cornerstones of a new world order. The secret to my freedom will be forgiving myself. Richard will be with me again, the angel assures me. The aching in my heart was so severe that becoming stone was a blessing – I could no longer feel the pain of Richard's death throughout the ensuing millennia.

Conquering my fear is the first step in my mission. Events in the exterior world are only fearful if they find resonance in my soul. Stone is rich and alive but it does not live. The many gems and crystals of the world may inspire and tune the human body to a purer vibration. That is why Eleanor comes to see me. She is strengthened by the simplicity and richness of the light emitted from my stone being. I am strengthened by her open heart and quiet mind.

Which way calls me? The way of the heart or the way of shame? There are many paths and all serve to teach the wayfarer. There are no mistakes. There are choices made at the time with the level of consciousness of the person in question. But I should have been wiser. I was privileged. I was guided by the finest in the realm. What happened? Why did I fail? Why did I act in discord with my true self?

Fear, self-loathing, and disgust fill my stone being.

Author speaks:

Clara will be the most famous statue in the world. Her example will awaken women and men to their true magnificence. Worldly success will be measured by the joy in following one's passion. And, even if not, the path chosen at the time would still be worthwhile through knowledge and wisdom gained. I made a few detours in my various careers but each one taught me something that proved useful much later in life. For example, in the 1980s I worked as a project assistant for a sports organisation and met a few Olympic athletes, then recent and veteran. They were all rigorous in their training and lifestyle. Quite a few were vegetarian, then considered a strange lifestyle. Meeting them taught me that even if I had natural talent, I would still need to train with consistency, develop the strength of character to overcome the many obstacles in my path, and make the necessary changes in habits and lifestyle. Success was never automatic.

In August 1987, at the Olympic stadium in Rome, with sixty thousand spectators, I witnessed a Canadian sprinter break the world record in the hundred metres. I can still feel the euphoria while writing this thirty-five years later. I met him briefly, later that year, at an awards gala in Monte Carlo. He seemed a sweet soul, lost and confused by sudden world-wide fame and recognition. The following year, at the Olympic Games in Seoul, his urine tests revealed steroids – a banned substance. He was disqualified and banned from competition. His new world record and gold medal were rescinded. I watched the Games from

London on television with my first husband, Gary. I cried so hard. My heart was broken. My young idealistic mind could not comprehend the lust for glory, endorsements, and marketing deals that shackled the heart of sport. Where was that drive to transcend human limits in clean competition?

The best athletes seemed to compete with, not against, each other.

I am grateful for all my career experiences, great and not so great. Clara chose me as her advocate in this world. Is she an imaginary friend? A voice in my heart from another dimension of space-time?

Was I losing my mind?

No.

Cocaine?

Narcotics have never interested me. I do not wish to run away from any reality I have created. My drugs of choice are green tea, fine chocolate, and an occasional half-bottle of Sicilian red wine – hardly strong enough to cause hallucinations. I cannot even tolerate caffeine in coffee.

In 2018, I attended a lecture in London given by a famous Hollywood screenwriter, a master of his craft. He stated that his eleven-p.m.-to-five-a.m. writing sessions were once fuelled by caffeine, nicotine, alcohol, and cocaine. He said the little people who lived in his typewriter needed those inducements to come out and play. He could get a lot of writing done. He wrote, among many screenplays, *Taxi Driver* (1976), a classic character-led film of crime and violence. I asked him whether he ever had writer's block. He replied that he was always a night writer but once his first child was born, going to bed at six a.m. intoxicated, no longer worked. He would go to an office each day and sit until, at last one day, the writing came. It took him a year to become a day writer.

It has taken me over twenty years to become any kind of writer; to learn that daily discipline in confronting my usual anxiety, not knowing what I'm doing until I sit and face the unknown next line which could be crap. But, I don't know, it's crap unless I let it breathe awhile on the laptop screen. My judgemental mind demands immediate logic and order in my writing. She demands that every line, every concept is clear as soon as I type them. She lives in a fantasy world. She is the mortal enemy of my artistic heart.

Usually, I distract my mind with instrumental music, a rich classical soundtrack from a film I've enjoyed. My mind relaxes its judgement mode, releasing my heart to play and make a mess. Writing is messy. A story never appears fully formed. It takes time to follow, investigate, and discover it until the whole story emerges, greater than the sum of its anchoring details.

A painter's discipline would be to face the blank canvas and allow the paint to tell the story. This allowing is surrender. This surrender is the discipline of transcending the demands of my judgemental mind, also known as my ego. For a brief period of time, the author does not seem to exist. The stillness of mind allows the story to unfold.

Stillness is not a passive state but one of focus and readiness for inspired action. The battle is always between inspiration and fear. Waiting is strength. The shadows lengthen, golden sunshine bathes the trees lush from days of heavy rain. It has been a beautiful day.

Clara speaks to the author:

Words do not ring true. All is confusion within the stone that is me. I have learned that a temporary state of confusion is healthy when I am defeating a limiting belief. Persisting in confusion is another matter: I must not avoid the responsibility of creating new empowering beliefs. Be patient with me. It is no fault of yours that today there are no words to write. I have been quiet for a few days, for good reason. A mind in flux has little of value to offer until it reconnects with the heart.

I feel your trust in me. My gratitude is immeasurable. Let the words rest in the stillness. Have no fear, they are neither stagnant nor are they dying. They are vibrant. Anxiety is a disease of the ego. Rest in the stillness. Feel the majesty of the silence within you.

All creativity comes from emptiness, from stillness. Motion and action may bring some motivation, but it takes stillness for the seeds of inspired action to take root and grow in the spirit.

Be ready for me. This is the practice. Be peaceful with the dry wordless days as those of delirious deluge. All is perfect. You are guided. This is the discipline: hold still while the storms of fears and doubt rage within you.

26

GOD KNOWS

~ Clara ~

For thousands of years I battled my demons in that cave in the mountains of southern Italy; demons of self-doubt, fear, remorse, anger, shame, and depression. They were my greatest teachers, second only to the Angel of Compassionate Condemnation who has been a constant companion since my death.

I had forgotten that an enlightened human being embraces all demons and transmutes their power by allowing them to rage in stillness until they are spent. That is all they had been trying to teach me. They succeeded only after I had been dead for twenty-five thousand years.

It has been a long journey. For the last hundred years my task has been to observe humanity and learn compassion for human weakness. Where once I was quick to anger at ignorance and spiritual waste, I learned to accept where each person was on their individual path even though I could see with searing clarity into their souls. I could see the light within them – their higher self's desire to flourish as who they truly were. Ignorance reigns when fear is great and self-knowledge is small. When I released my anger without harm to anyone, I gained peace. I had passed harsh judgement on those whose only crime was to remind me of my own many shortcomings. When I waged war in my inner world, I could only see war in my outer world.

As it is within, so it is without.

If I find peace within, my outer-world reality becomes peace. I have learned that my greatest gift to humanity is compassion, especially towards my enemy, Xoran who is now James. I once feared him: he reminded me of shame so deep it chilled me to my bones. He, too, has been a great teacher. My painful task is to confront the lies lurking in the shadows of my spirit. I now understand why I needed to become stone, to take refuge in the glistening stillness of marble.

Today all is light. My dark shadows are now friends who remind me to practise compassion. I pray you do not suffer as I have. I pray you are bestowed with a vast spiritual intelligence and that your heart resonates with joy.

Indeed, this is your birthright.

27

WAITING

~ Clara ~

I wish I could show you the steps to healing, but every statue is different and yet we are all the same. For some statues it was unbearable grief that had them seek refuge in stone. For others it was a burning anger or rage, or horror. For me, it was shame, remorse, and disgust for my past. Compassion is the key to unlocking all our private hells.

Every day I see many statues in human form. Their hearts became stone within their bodies of flesh and bone. They experienced so much trauma their hearts simply shut down. They preferred to feel nothing and live in oblivion instead of flowing in the full richness of life in all its joys and sorrows.

Stillness awash in love releases all old stories and traumas from the past. I am beginning to feel this stillness. It is rich. It is deep. It is satisfying. All judgement and condemnation fades from my being just as the Angel of Compassionate Condemnation promised.

The late afternoon sun warms my stone form. I radiate heat and light. That's how Eleanor finds me in the park. She can see me glowing near the redwoods. The anger has faded away to reveal sadness but that, too, has flowed out of me with grace.

Emotions are the centre of human existence. There are peaceful ways to express dark emotions. The sacred words are spoken and emotions fade to reveal joy. I await the words from the poet, promised by the angel. I cannot accomplish this alone.

I love those deep red damask roses. I have forgotten their perfume. They grew wild in the gardens of my palace and along the walls of my mountain retreat. And now, again, they grow around my plinth. No matter how I close myself off from life, the wild power of love always finds me, whether through kind words from a thoughtful friend, a lover's caress, a beautiful flower. Life is worth living for these experiences alone.

My ancestors had long forgiven me. I had brought disgrace to my august family line, but they assured me all had been in accordance with divine plans. I thank God no records of my former life exist today. I have learned that compassion begins with oneself. The hardest task has been to find forgiveness for myself within my heart of stone and to accept what I have done. I can hear the waves of the ocean in its distant hypnotic dance; the slow retreat, the rolling advance, and the crashing surrender on the shores. A plaintive lover's unceasing caress of his beloved cursed to crumble into the ocean depths if she dares to requite his love.

Surrendering to love would crumble my formidable defences. No one can hear me today. The sacred words do not flow from my heart. Words heal when spoken because they resonate with the treasury of golden words in the heart – the ones that were always there but I could not hear them for I was not ready.

A word can strike a chord when the body and spirit are tuned to hear them whether for transfiguration or degradation. But, in all of this, I see neither good nor bad.

Each one of us has a unique path to follow. An evil person may teach us all to awaken and discern, to remind us who we really are by showing us who we are not. I pray for Xoran because his path seems Godforsaken and his duty thankless. His actions taught me to listen to my intuitive mind; to trust the wisdom from my heart, no matter how illogical or irrational that wisdom may seem to my rational mind.

As the earth ascends to a new consciousness, those of evil intent will no longer incarnate unless we fail to grasp the lessons they have brought us.

I am not helpless unless I choose to believe so. I am endowed with free will, but at times I do not realise the power I possess

I created my private hell: my individual creation of lessons and experiences repeated with no learning and no growth – an endless cycle – unbroken unless a blessed being is invoked and sacred prayers recited.

To be born human is a privileged incarnation. Even enlightened beings return lifetime after lifetime to help their fellow humans ascend to their true greatness – aspects of divine source.

Life is a dance. Find our own rhythm and attract those moving to the same or multiples of time.

A clue to one's private hell is the recurrence of unresolved drama in one's life just as in my own. I was unable to forgive myself; I feared my enemy, Xoran. I was unable to face him and seize my responsibility in the story. He has been a brutal, formidable teacher.

No story is worth telling unless one of the characters grows and their journey reaches a resolution that satisfies the patient listener and reader. The story tells the author when it is complete and ready to be told. The author is the last to know despite years spent of writing, editing, and rewriting.

My journey remains incomplete, but I am joyful even though the journey has been hard to bear. I have excellent company in my chosen storyteller. She abandoned a career in banking to follow a far riskier path with me. At times she has been hard on herself too. No one is perfect according to human order thinking or mindset. In the thinking of a divine order, however, we are all perfect in our imperfections: they are jewels lodged in our souls before birth. They indicate the paths of grace we chose in the life to come.

Do not pass harsh judgement on ourselves. Cease all condemnation. Celebrate the life we have now. To love is to accept. To forgive is to accept, but not condone, what has happened and willingly heal from the suffering. Forgiveness is not dependent on the perpetrator's remorse. Granting forgiveness is our bid for freedom.

28

MERCY

~ Clara ~

Mercy is clear. It demands no reason, no payment. It sees into the heart and acts. It is swayed by neither anger, rage, nor fury. Mercy brings peace to all. Mercy takes place when there is compassion; therefore, compassion is the key to peace.

An empress understands these principles: she is slow to war and quick to peace. A realm's resources cannot be replenished as easily as they are lost in war.

Even though I invoked him at my death, the Angel of Compassionate Condemnation is an angel of mercy. His desire is that I gain this quality and release myself from suffering. An angel can be of assistance only with my permission. Otherwise, they stand by in infinite compassion and love, awaiting my heartfelt request for their intervention. Human beings are all encoded with grace. The angels may help us decipher our unique code.

Gratitude overwhelms me. It is the most powerful of emotions because it is the first sign of healing. Who is the poet? It is Eleanor who visits me here in San Francisco. I have not seen her for a while. In a world of confusion and darkness it is difficult to maintain a clear mind and a strong heart without spiritual training. Eleanor has worked with discipline and dedication despite many setbacks and crises of faith. She grows stronger each day. No matter how far away she is, Aurora finds her and watches over her too. On occasion, a silken feather will fly in Aurora's wake. She may even leave behind a flight feather as a visiting card. Such physical evidence is a rare and auspicious event.

It is Aurora's blessing.

In a few years' time, Eleanor will wonder at the deep red velvet roses growing at will around her garden. On warm days she will hear the unfurling and beating of large wings and wonder why they sound familiar. A woman's usual instinctive response would be alarm at the sound of a large predatory creature flying in the vicinity of her home. Yet, she will feel at ease leaving her infant daughter asleep in the garden. The gentle Japanese maples shade the infant from the afternoon sun; their delicate leaves whisper a sweet lullaby in the summer breeze.

Any child is a precious sign of mercy.

29

A Meditation on Romance

~ Eleanor ~

I love the chemistry of getting to know a man confident in who he is and who he is not. He exudes, above all else, a quiet strength, kindness, and intelligence. But chemistry is not enough to guarantee happiness. Do we share the same values of honesty and integrity? Compatible character traits? Allied life paths?

Without answers to those questions, any love affair I start is doomed, both parties wondering what went wrong, or worse still, blaming the other for their unhappiness. My crime was to believe the lies my former lover told me. He wanted "a farm of children" he said, but once we sexually bonded, he simply changed his mind.

No relationship can survive when fundamental agreements are broken.

I am guilty by omission: I chose a man who was much older than me; I chose a man who had had a vasectomy that may or may not have been reversible. I did not leave him as soon as he changed his mind. I didn't leave until eighteen months later. I wasted that time trying to accommodate his wishes and subjugating my own. The consequence of my inaction at a critical time is that today my children are unconceived, unborn. They do not exist.

I had forgotten I have a life and purpose too. When did my instinct to nurture and accommodate others become poisoned with resentment and anger? I failed to take care of my needs. I failed to speak up because I believed it was not my right to do so: a clear sign of lack of self-esteem. I had set myself up for failure. Why? What has been the point of all this struggle? To eventually help others?

I feel too old now. I have lost faith in myself.

I remember being naked in our bed, my arms and legs wrapped around him.

'Oh yes, yes, yes.' My voice was hoarse with pleasure.

'Shut up.' His rhythmic pelvic thrust had stopped for a moment, reptilian eyes stared into mine. I never thought pale blue could be so cold, so dead. He resumed fucking me. I never knew who he was making love to in his mind. It certainly wasn't me.

I no longer care.

Why do I feel powerless and stupid? Why do I always feel angry?

Is this the anger of awakening that Clara talked about in our conversations? I swear I do not know how I would have survived these dark years without her. When I sat by her plinth in the wisteria gazebo in Kew Gardens, I felt a peace within me like no other. I missed her when she moved to San Francisco. It did not take long to rearrange my life, to leave London, and be near her again in a whole new world.

Why did she move to San Francisco? What would she gain by being there instead of England? This is not for me to reason why. There may be events unfolding that require my willingness to surrender and play my part in the human drama. There may be events unfolding of which Clara is ignorant for her own protection.

Clara taught me to trust and have faith at a time in my life when I had become bitter. I feel her near me always. When I feel lost and empty she reminds me to look for a quiet message or a sign timed to perfection: It may be in the form of an email, a song playing in the sound system of a shop or café, a message on social media, a conversation with a stranger, an article in the press, a passage in a book.

Communicating with Clara can feel overwhelming. Some days I feel chaotic inside. Clara advises me to let the storms pass, take no action, and be a compassionate observer of my internal state. New learnings and insights need time to integrate into my growing consciousness. Every realisation will release deep emotions that are transient as a cloud drifting across a spring sky.

Thoughts are energy.

Patterns of thoughts give rise to patterns of energy or emotions in my being. Is it possible that some unconscious energy patterns may not be due to disempowering beliefs? What if they are imprints from another lifetime that furthers the evolution of my soul in the present lifetime?

Clara would know the answer to these questions. I dared not ask her; she seemed troubled. I wonder what makes her heart so heavy with pain? I hope to gain her trust, to share and lighten her suffering. My recent heartbreak and temporary identity crisis are nothing beside whatever she has endured.

Statues reveal their secrets slowly, if at all. Crystalline stone, like marble, is a good keeper of secrets. I am honoured to be Clara's friend.

What is my friendship with Clara? I love her as a friend and confidante. I do not tell acquaintances that I visit a statue in Golden Gate Park. Some people are afraid of the unusual and the unexplained.

The path to my sanity exposed the insanity in my environment. Some may choose to believe fixed ideas as I once did. I would attack ideas that contradicted my view of reality rather than incorporate them into my evolving consciousness. This rigidity of thought led to rigidity of my consciousness and debate, my growth stalled and I could feel myself dying inside.

Clara speaks of compassion. I can see why it is so important today. So much suffering results from restricted, conditioned consciousness. My higher self knows that I have a divine birthright to enjoy both spiritual and material wealth, but somehow the manifestation of this birthright was thwarted. I could not see any other way beyond my limiting beliefs. I could only see what I believed after all.

I used to fret I was deficient or dysfunctional in some way and therefore accepted that life was going to be a struggle from an early age. I now see these negative beliefs are not unique to me but are universal, limiting beliefs that trap the spirits and souls of my fellow human beings.

Perhaps, I may now have compassion for the gentlemen who attempted to woo me, a woman of deep frozen emotions. May I never again cause pain in a man because of my inability to respond to his romantic overtures.

Romance is not dead.

I was.

What changed? What has been my transformation? A choice to withdraw and refocus my life on my own destiny, independent of any path that depends on romantic fulfilment. If a woman chases romance, it runs away. If a woman is still, vibrant, resolute in her values, she cannot help but attract the passionate pursuit of romance. The stillness in a woman is the pure feminine principle that shines through her body. She becomes the manifestation of the universal goddess.

Why the epidemic of depression among mature women today? Why, as they approach their prime, are they afflicted with this terrible illness? Have I been brainwashed into believing that material success, marriage, and children are what I was meant to dream about? Is this depression really a suppressed anger that I was too afraid to own? Have I been cheated into believing that only shopping for things and mechanical sex will make me happy?

No matter how many shoes, clothes, and handbags I can buy, no matter how many lovers I can attract, without a true spiritual awakening I will only feel more empty and disconnected than ever before.

Men love beautiful women. Women love beautiful things. Both attempt to access the divine beyond the beauty and promise of status beheld. However, the trinkets and trappings of external wealth cannot relieve the hunger for internal spiritual wealth, that deep sense of inner peace and purpose, being in the zone, the oneness of all.

Sages throughout history advocated decades and lifetimes of spiritual training with a teacher or master. Today, in the early 21st century, human consciousness is evolving so fast that daily meditation and prayer is vital to maintain sanity despite the many duties of family, work, pressures from government, and deliberate messages of confusion from a controlled media.

The duties that were once a burden become a way to experience the divine. I could see the mystical in the mundane: loading the dishwasher as an expression of love for my family; when my family had a giant dog, a walk in the park was a miraculous experience, his shaggy white fur bright in the morning mist; a business meeting becomes an opportunity to make the world a better place for everyone. There is a deep stillness in every action taken and a vibrancy in the stillness of every moment.

A spiritual practice allows me pause for reflection and cultivates that stillness – brain and body are alert, awake, in gentle readiness. For example, going out for a solitary run or sitting in meditation brings to light unresolved issues and thoughts hidden behind the routine rush of the workday.

Clara is an outsider. So am I. We do not live conventional lives and so it is easier to observe and witness the human condition. The duty of an artist and poet is to live a marginal existence, bringing these abstract observations into the mainstream human experience through the emotional power of their art – the abstract made real.

Works of art, whether a painting, a sculpture, a piece of music, a piece of writing, a film or a play, can provide an experience of a whole new world by articulating emotions people feel but could neither accept nor resolve until the work of art appeared. Mass transformation of human belief systems causes an awakening: new actions are taken and the world is forever changed. For example, a marine biologist, dying of cancer, wrote a book on the dangers of pesticides. Rachel Carson's *Silent Spring* caused a furore in 1962 and sparked a worldwide movement.

I was born into a community and shaped by their beliefs. I chose to unlearn many beliefs otherwise my growth would have stalled. Beliefs like, "You can't trust anyone" or, "You cannot have everything" did not serve me. I deliberately neglected one subject at school so I could fail the exam because I believed it was not possible to pass all the exams. I took on too many subjects at university, failed to manage the schedule of lectures and assignments, and consequently failed my second-year exams. I repeated the year and gained my degree.

An education that encourages students to think for themselves, wise teachers, a quest for lifelong learning and growth, allow a student to become their true self while still respecting the traditions of their family and culture. Traditions die if they become too rigid. Communities die if they do not evolve with rising human consciousness.

Today we see clashes with those who seek to control the evolution of their people by enforcing adherence to outworn interpretations of religious texts, missing the eternal message of compassion and destroying the contribution of the feminine.

The vast majority of people want to live in harmony. In prosperous cities, people of many faiths and cultures live side by side in peace, with mosques, temples, churches, and synagogues near each other on the same city meridian. I grew up in such a place in south London. I could see how the consciousness of the people was reflected in the environment. Healthy trees reflect prosperity in a city.

I loved living in London until I betrayed my dreams by settling for a relationship with an unsuitable man. Every building, every street corner, every road, bridge, bus, train would remind me of my time with him, the time now lost and the time that will never be regained. I could no longer bear the memories laden in the city of stone.

I came to San Francisco to find Clara again and to awaken the woman I could have been. Nobody knows why bad things happen. It's naïve to believe I had any control. Of course, now, with hindsight, I see I could have made wiser choices before and during the doomed affair. At what point did I betray myself? Why did I ignore my intuition? I ignored the humiliation I felt because I believed I was too sensitive. I preferred to listen to my false reason as he openly flirted with a female friend. I dishonoured my intuition long before my lover dishonoured me.

Clara speaks to Eleanor:

'Acknowledge your error and forgive yourself. It will release you from bondage. You acted to the best of your consciousness at the time. Welcome that painful time. It allowed a powerful awakening in you.' Clara's voice was always a beacon of light in the darkness of my thoughts.

'Are you saying I should be grateful for such pain and humiliation?'

'No. You could be grateful. How you feel is your choice and your choice alone. That painful experience led you to your path today. It was a necessary corrective measure called into your life by your soul's longing for a divine awakening while in a human experience.'

'I've lost so many years in getting my confidence back.'

'Those years saved you from far greater suffering. No time is lost when it is used in the pursuit of learning and growth.'

'Clara, I don't know if I am willing to risk falling in love again.'

'Trust who you are now, Eleanor. Trust who you are today, for you have come far. The woman you were, the woman you fear you may still be, is no more.'

'So much time wasted in pain and regret. I didn't realise until now that I was also healing and growing in consciousness. What do I do now?'

'Take one step at a time. Trust your intuition and invent each action as you proceed on your path. Do not, under any circumstances, heed the voices of fear whether they emanate from you or from anyone else.'

'How can I tell the voices of fear from those of love? Sometimes the voices of fear seem rational and sensible which makes them hard to ignore.'

'An astute observation, Eleanor. Heeding a voice of fear creates a sinking feeling in your heart and shuts down your life force. You may feel a constriction in your belly and perhaps back pain too. You may feel the effects of the voice of fear in your body because you are not a statue. A voice of fear seeks to exert control by promising safety and security – those great illusions that imprison many souls – cutting off the flow of divine guidance. A voice of love, however, seeks to free your being to the ecstasy of unfolding miracles that is divine energy. You may feel fear as exhilaration because your heart will feel open, curious, and even excited by the adventure. A voice of love would always advise you to let go and allow yourself to become a work of art.'

'What is the purpose of my individual will?'

'Your will is your conscious choice to surrender, or not, to your higher self, that part of you connected to divine source. During your human experience it is to be expected that you lose your connection on occasion. Your will helps you connect and reconnect through prayer, meditation, and through works that alleviate the suffering of others.'

'How do these practices help?'

'They focus and quieten the mind to allow the heart to speak. In western civilisation of the present era, we have given supremacy to the rational mind which has been useful in overcoming superstition and birthing scientific advancements of recent centuries. However, today, the rational mind, devoid of any visionary intuition, has proven bankrupt. In an enlightened age, the rational mind serves, not ignores, the heart. The consequences of ignoring the heart are fatal.'

'Does this mean heart disease would disappear as the leading cause of death in the western world?'

'A healthy calm mind means a vibrant heart and a radiant body. Following the heart rejuvenates one's whole being.'

Clara's words seem alien but there is no denying their wisdom. Her ideas make sense to me. Perhaps I am going crazy and losing touch with reality, but what is reality anyway? An agreement by society to take on a set of values, opinions, and norms? To tolerate chronic stress and unhappiness as a normal way to live? I wish I had the wisdom and the courage to transcend these strictures. There's got to be more to life than this.

'The very fact you are aware and have the desire to transform is the first step to discovering your path. It only takes a little courage to find the next step on your path. On the way, as you gather momentum, you will find more courage and the means to continue, for this is sacred law.'

As usual, Clara could read my heart. Wisdom and compassion flowed from her marble being. I always felt at peace sitting by her plinth. The perfume of the vibrant red roses would slow the flow of time. My thoughts would become lucid, as though blessed with an intelligence tempered by eternity.

I did not care whether Clara was imaginary or real. I did not care what others might have thought. She was real in my heart and that was all that mattered.

'Eleanor, you have been in my dreams for thousands of years. You have been real for me long before you were born in this lifetime.'

30

DIVINE LOVE

~ Clara ~

When love appears as a romantic partner, a new energy sparks between the lovers. It is as though their energies resonate in recognition and celebration. We may be destined to meet one or more soulmates in our lifetimes. Each one is our teacher, showing us an aspect of who we really are.

When I am lost from my inner source of wisdom, I am in discord. Love reminds me who I really am. Love will stand for my soul's highest expression, regardless of the circumstances or how weak my faith.

The angels all around us have this love for us. Their earnest desire is that we embrace and receive love to reveal and express our natural talents and gifts.

In a world of darkness and confusion, love is the guiding light through the many paths of fear. The art is to discover this infinite source of love within ourselves. Tap into this source and you will never be lost in fear again.

Take an inspired step, flow and relax while in action, known in some athletic disciplines as "being in the zone". There may be chaos around you, there may be discontent and sadness, but you will see and understand that those paths are also chosen. You will have compassion, too, and continue on your path without fear.

I now know why I made many grave errors: I was a fool. I had made all my decisions from fear. I did not act from the abundant love and truth in my heart. I had become too preoccupied with duties of state and had ceased my daily meditation and spiritual practices. These had kept me centred and connected to my deepest intuition and wisdom. Instead, I became vulnerable to the lies and deceit growing around me in my court administration. It is clear now how far I had strayed in the ensuing storms of fear and doubt. Many died as a consequence of my misrule.

'They forgave you long before their death,' said the Angel of Compassionate Condemnation, 'They are all at peace and pray for you without end.' His mighty presence was infinite gentleness.

'For me?' I failed to understand my heavenly companion. 'Lost armies of fine women and men pray for me?'

He closed his eyes to affirm and smiled with his usual quiet majesty. He radiated infinite love and peace. A new light infused my marble being. A new strength filled my fractured heart.

'They pray that you find peace within yourself for your destiny is yet to be revealed.' His magnificent wings enveloped me in blessing; a glistening palace of silken platinum energy streams fell from above my head to the ground and beyond. He had submerged his forty-foot-tall luminous form deep into the ground behind me so that his heart was closer to mine. The ground became a calm grassy sea with only the upper third of this form visible. The trees were happy; the angel had touched and healed their fragile roots.

The ache in my heart subsided. Deep in the core of my being, the cold tight feeling faded away. Even though I was still stone, I now had a strange freedom to give and receive light. I was no longer locked in tension and closed off from the world around me. I was free to give and receive love.

31

PEACE

~ Clara ~

'Find peace within you,' said the angel. 'There can be no peace without justice, no justice without trust and faith. Find the infinite source of love within you. Bring yourself to justice without condemnation and you will win peace. All sadness and grief arise when you are disconnected from whom you truly are.'

'If I work only on myself, of what use it is to anyone else?' I said.

'When you work to clarify and enlighten yourself, your energetic vibration rises and you cannot help but heal others around you.'

As in the usual order of our conversations, the angel's words resonate throughout my stone form. I am blessed to have him by my side. Statues need angelic guidance too. The Diablo winds have brought fine ash from the forest fires north of the bay. As a consequence, these past few days, the sun has become a brilliant fuchsia globe, mesmerising all those who gaze upon the star low on the horizon, the ocean aflame in pink and lavender hues. I cannot see the star as my view is fixed facing east. I surmise the beauty of these recent sunsets by the cherry blossom pink glow of my white marble form. Here, it seems, I both absorb and transmit light.

Even though I cannot watch the daily gift of sunset, I imagine an ephemeral art installation of the grandest scale. The city is bathed in a surreal light that calms the many hyper-analytical minds of my beloved San Franciscans.

I have been touched by death all my life. I lived with vibrancy and passion only when I accepted my own mortality. I may seem mortal now, but I do not live as a human being. My limitations are not from fear of external circumstances. My ego died long ago. Only my heart knows that circumstances can be transcended and created to realise one's dreams, even those of a statue.

My hyper-rational mind was frightened by a heart that seemed wild and dangerous in its intuitive guidance. My heart holds the key to divine communication, but my mind did not trust the guidance coming through. I now know that any human mind is by nature limited. It cannot see all possibilities but must serve the all-knowing heart even if the next suggested action seems difficult. My mind was not at peace. It was unwell, swayed by the immediate concerns and needs of my ego: being in command, in control, feeling safe. My dreams were easily abandoned, causing life force to ebb from my body into rapid ageing and decay.

A still mind is not a passive mind. It is alert to intuition. It is wise. An awakened heart communicates with little effort to the wise mind. Resistance by an unwell mind wastes precious life force. It has taken me thousands of years in my refuge of stone to quell my ignorant resistance and glimpse liberation.

Today, an undercurrent of human compassion has emerged all over the world. The insanity of war and our beautiful planet's destruction are questioned by many human beings who now work in collaboration, not competition, with each other.

'You underestimate your part, o wise one,' said the angel. He had appeared, as usual, while I was deep in thought. He appears by my side with neither fanfare nor heavenly proclamation. In the early years following my death, I would be frightened by his sudden appearances. It took me five thousand years to grow accustomed to his immense power and presence. I now draw comfort from his strength, compassion, and gentleness. At this time, I could find no reply worthy of my friend and companion. I accepted his words in silence.

In the beginning was the word.

I sometimes fail to comprehend the power of that phrase. When words are pronounced by a being with coherent energy frequencies, the world described by those words will manifest.

What is a being of coherent energies?

One whose thoughts, words, and actions are aligned. If one speaks of love but has thoughts of fear or hatred, the person is energetically fractured and their power of intention scattered and unfocused. How can I be at peace with another if I am at war within myself?

I have spent millennia in stone yet I know nothing. My intellectual mind once craved the certainty of ordered knowledge and structure. My heart, instead, has the intelligence to surrender to the mystery.

My dreams are deep. Sometimes they float into my consciousness. I cannot manifest my dreams in their true glory. So much hunger and desire without power to assuage them. Pity the statues of ancient worlds, our features worn down by aeons of time, the succeeding ages unable to discern our once exquisite forms. In a thousand years I may become yet another broken statue, of little or no consequence.

32

A LITTLE PIECE OF HELL

~ Memoir ~ Author ~

21:39 GMT, Monday 11 February 2008: What in hell's name am I doing here on this earth? What am I doing here? Why was I born? I feel useless. I have lived a wasted life. What have I achieved in this lifetime? I am forty-six years old and I am tired of being alive.

Reading through old writings from 2004 onwards proved a depressing enterprise. I should have just re-read the writings of 2007 – the first draft. There seems to be two books intertwined like conjoined twins. Was Clara once destined to have been my twin sister? Did she send me to incarnate alone instead? But I am instead blessed with my younger sister and confidante, M.

I have been yearning for the divine all my life. Clara has never left me but I have not been aware of her until now. She reassures me that this discomfort and uncertainty is simply the death of an old version of me, the author. I have never been so fat or so poor in all of my life.

23:53 GMT, Monday continued: A strange day of cleansing and reading over old documents from the "Statue" folder in my notebook computer. The headaches have subsided.

It was a mistake to read over some of the older writings. The dreams and desires there have not been fulfilled. The writings seem full of complaint and self-loathing. I cannot live any longer that way. There must be a better way short of death? The final release? But, I would have failed in my mission and would need to be born again to repeat the whole bloody cycle of trauma, anxiety and depression.

The word acceptance comes to me now. Accept that I am always going to be depressed at times? No, but I wonder if this is a special anniversary of a time that I have forgotten? The last time I felt this low was last November, on the tenth anniversary of my divorce being finalised. Perhaps there was a similar anniversary around this time. I do not remember, but clearly my body does. All I can feel is hopelessness, sadness and uselessness. The pain is the same – feeling lost and emotionally disembowelled. This old energy coming up to be healed. I cannot live any longer if this is to continue. It seems to happen every few weeks. I don't think I can live any longer with these recurring bouts of depression. There is no anxiety at least, it's more a resignation that nothing I do makes any difference. No matter what I do, I will just get fatter, poorer, older and the book will still be incomplete, taunting me as a mirage in a desert.

Clara says I need to experience this dark time of my soul otherwise how could I have compassion for the pain of others? Also, how could I show others the way out of their shadows unless I have experienced my own empowerment? I forget that deep transformation is not always comfortable.

Enough for now.

I feel better already. Thank you, Clara.

13:00 GMT, Tuesday 12 February 2008: Feeling lighter and brighter today. The depression is passing. I understand that the sadness and sense of loss is symptomatic of a deep transformation. Old beliefs are dying inside me; old beliefs such as being unworthy of love and success unless I make some valiant superhuman effort to prove myself worthy and to compensate for my many perceived flaws.

But Clara sent me herself to live in this world of shame and sadness. I am her spy, an agent charged with the impossible mission of mass transformation. I cannot fail unless I believe the brainwashing of this external, so-called, real world. Clara sent me herself. She trusts me with this mission. I must not fail her. I have always been worthy and deserving. I believed the lies of this world. My spirit is finally clearing these old shadows. I must be patient as my spirit emerges and soars to its authentic place of expression.

The book will unfold as these shadows pass. In the meantime, take care of myself and nurture my whims and needs. Listen to what my body needs. My body is expressing the desires from my soul.

It will take some practice to listen to, and speak from my heart. I have been so accustomed to ignoring my real feelings and speaking from a rational and empty stratosphere detached from my soul. Is it any wonder I have no success in manifesting my deepest desires?

My new husband never appeared. My children were never conceived, never born. My fertile years wasted.

What now?

Patience as the shadows pass from my soul, revealing my divine source. I have been anxious to hear Clara's voice but I can see now that her voice would have been lost in the morass of lies cloaking my heart. It is a lie that I am unworthy of love and success. It is a lie that I am loser in life. I am alive. I have an important contribution to make in this world. I am here to bring prosperity and peace.

From the book *Autobiography of a Yogi* by Paramahamsa Yogananda, I learned that spiritual and material wealth can coexist. In fact, without spiritual wealth, material wealth is worthless. A part of me is dying. I feel it is important to note the passing of the old, and to celebrate the new emerging being. Maybe, it is wise to commemorate the passing of the old with a kind of funeral.

14:13 GMT, Tuesday continued: a gorgeous day. Grateful for the sunshine these past two days. It may have saved my life. I am truly blessed. The shadows across my heart are lifting. I will be free to be my true self and fulfil my destiny.

Desires create karma by some universal law where all heartfelt desires must find fulfilment in human lifetimes. This karma will keep me coming back to new lifetimes and keep me trapped in the cycle of life and death.

'Clara, what did you do to escape this suffering?'

'I had faith that if any desire I had was unfulfilled then it was for a higher reason unknown to me at the time.'

'You could let the desire go so easily?'

'Yes, I just let it go, allowing new desires to take its place. Holding on to a desire then denying it creates shadows in the heart and much suffering to the soul.'

'So, telling the truth to myself about all my desires allows them to come to light and be released to the glory of the universe?'

'This is the writing faith. Stand firm with a soft and open heart. Clear the thoughts from your troubled mind by writing them down as they appear. Witness them but do not dwell on them; all the complaints and the fears. They will heal as you write them.' Clara is clear and calm as always.

My greatest fear is that I will never finish this book because of some secret inadequacy of mine. These are silent assassins of a fulfilled life – the limiting beliefs deep in my subconscious world. I am afraid I will never find even moderate success in contributing my talents to the world and making a decent living. If it were not for my parents' generosity, I do not know what I would have done.

I saw a possible future where I had become a mediocre investment banker. My heart was no longer in that profession. I would have grown in cynicism and depression. I saw a possible future where my career success was fuelled by a growing dependency on alcohol, cocaine, or prescription opiate drugs, as usual among some colleagues. The alcohol and drugs would have medicated the pain of disconnection from my true path.

All the wonderful resort locations in the world, all the lavish material things money could buy would not satisfy the desire to write a book and fulfil my true mission.

I am on my path. It is not always easy, but it is far better than lying to myself. There is no point trying to be anyone else but me.

I had shut down my feelings because I feared their depths and power to overwhelm me, but now I understand that my emotions are the navigational tool of a rich inner life. I had amputated the desires from my soul because the pain of denying them was far less than the pain of being unable to fulfil them. Amputating feelings brought me nothing but a dead life. I did a great job in denying the depths of my hurt or joy in my earlier life and wondered why I was unable to manifest any of my dreams.

Telling myself the truth of how I feel and locating where in my body the emotion emanates helped me connect and dissolve that anger, sorrow, or joy. Only then, can the emotion be released and I can learn and grow from the experience. From what I have learned, emotions and feelings are supposed to flow through my body like a wave in an ocean. With emotions locked down there could be no room for new experiences. My body would be held in a statue-like vice of numbness and ineffectuality leading to depression.

Grateful for the brief ray of sunshine this afternoon after the rain, I trust Clara: write whatever comes and it will all fall into place. All it takes is to write from a heart full of compassion. The story will come alive again very soon.

There have been limiting beliefs that I had to deal with in myself to clear the channels for communication with the divine at regular, structured times instead of occasional moments of lucidity and peace. Clara speaks of writing while in a trance, alert yet in quiet wonder and surrender, with neither judgement nor condemnation of the words coming through.

My current consciousness may not always comprehend. It is for me to feel only and not rely on my rational mind to explain and analyse. That is the recourse of my old self, who would rather analyse than feel the story coming through. The story is beyond my rational mind. It would be a waste of time trying to intellectualise my way through the jungles of writing this book. If I listen to my heart I can see that the predators lurking in the darkness are only projections of my flaws that I have long denied. Embrace those shadows as they want to be accepted and loved.

17:38 GMT, Thursday 28 February 2008: I have lived so long divorced from what my heart says that it seems I need to break open a bank vault to access my true feelings. Feelings are not comfortable, but it is through the darkness of the repressed parts of me that I will know God, or rather my divine friend, Clara.

I am happy. Whatever strange sensations I experience now through writing and meditation, I understand are part of my spiritual growth and an unfolding process. I can minimise resistance and suffering by being watchful and observing emotions like anger, resentment, and ensuing depression with detachment, understanding they are coming from me and like me, they are passing. Nothing is permanent. I am not a victim of some outside circumstance nor some vile, capricious god. There is order in the seeming chaos of life. The darkness I had wilfully suppressed in me, until now, is the chaos.

12:09 GMT, Friday 29 February 2008: A cold grey day. I am hungry for spring but seasons cannot and must not be rushed just because they seem unpleasant to me. My neighbour's pear tree is bursting with promise, each branch and twig proud with nodules of new life, constellations of pale green stars dancing in the wind. Look for new life within me. The winds of darkness may be howling within me, but I let them pass. They cannot drown out the voice of God for long. This is faith: the understanding that all is well and always has been.

14:03 GMT, Friday continued: look for the sunshine behind the grey veil of illusion within me. The light is within. Look for God within. Do not fear the darkness as it is only a veil of separation – the ultimate illusion that we are separate, individual, and alone.

Author's notes, April 2022–September 2023
1. On the adventures of becoming a writer:

In the 2000s I struggled to write. I relied on my rational, logical mind. I tried to write a book, a work of the imagination, from the mindset of an investment banker. I would dismiss leaps of the imagination as nonsense. Only after a major heartbreak, at the end of a romantic relationship in 2003, did my ego finally let go. I would sit for an hour or two and feel these strange words coming through my fingertips. I did not comprehend what I was writing and became frightened by the interdimensional communication with the muse I came to know as Clara.

For example, I had the fixed idea to write Clara's story from the third person limited point of view, the fashion then for many published novels. Clara insisted first person omniscient was the way to go. It took me five years to see sense. The first draft of this book was not completed until April 2009. I sent the manuscript via courier to an agent in New York. I had met her during a "pitch-slam" event there four years earlier, a kind of speed-dating for literary agents and authors. That was an emotional experience for me. I was a wreck. I found speaking from my heart almost impossible in a business meeting.

I had made a complete fool of myself at the courier centre in central London that sunny April day in 2009. I handed over my manuscript in its green A4 folder to the gentleman associate and paid the fee. I tried not to cry. I asked him if I could take the package back for a moment. I held the manuscript against my heart one more time and breathed deeply. I am grateful still for the patience of that gracious employee at the FedEx ShipCenter, 114 Strand.

Outside, I walked towards Covent Garden and stopped outside the Embassy of Zimbabwe. I couldn't breathe. I called my sister on my mobile.

'I've done it. I've let her go. Clara is on a plane to New York tonight. She's all alone.'

My sister was sympathetic and supportive as always. Any passerby would have assumed I was a mother who had boarded her infant on a transatlantic flight as an unaccompanied minor.

The next day, once my drama-queen self had calmed down, I thought perhaps my manuscript had suffered two weaknesses at that time: one, too much exposition; two, Eleanor's character was too faint, not fully formed.

The New York literary agent's assistant emailed me four weeks later:

"Thank you for sending MEMOIRS OF A FORMER STATUE. Your premise is certainly intriguing, but I'm sorry to say we didn't feel quite as passionate about the narrative as we had hoped. Specifically, Eleanor wasn't entirely dimensional for us, and the writing was a bit exposition-heavy for our taste.

We sincerely appreciate the chance to review your work, and wish you the best in finding the perfect home for it."

There it was, clear as day: my writing and editing instincts were validated by a world-class publishing professional. Rejection was heartbreaking but enlightening too. On the bright side, I was on the right track. I just had more work to do. I changed the title back to *Meditations of a Former Statue*.

In the intervening years, I learned to write from the mindset and heartset of an artist. An artist requires even more discipline than my former banker self could possibly conceive. How could playing with new ideas be so hard? I took myself far too seriously, concerned others would judge me a loser, and not knowing who I was anymore. A true artist does not care. They take their work seriously, not worrying about how they may seem to others. My ego was my weakness.

I am still learning to trust the leaps of my imagination and intuition. Each day it gets a bit easier. Each day the leaps get a bit bigger.

2. On Family and Three Cultures:

Even though my sister and I were born and grew up in London, England, we are blessed with two more heritages. Ma came from the mountains of southern Italy while our father came from the flood plains and jungles of Bengal in northern India. The parents met in London and married in 1960. They remained married until Ma's death in 2020. My dad said they were soulmates.

My sister and I could not be categorised on English government forms. Our ethnicity was an unusual combination then: white Caucasian and Asian Indian. We looked unusual among London's mainly Caucasian population of the 1960s and 1970s. I remember attracting genuine curiosity destabilising the covert hostility usually reserved for my darker-skinned schoolmates of Pakistani, Indian, or Caribbean descent. Today, beautiful children of blended races are a common sight in London.

Italian and Indian-Bengali cultures share similar strong family ties, cuisines rich in herbs and spices, musical spoken languages, ancient civilisations, and colourful religions steeped in ceremonial magic. Hindus have many deities, each with their own ancient myths and legends. Roman Catholics have many saints, each with their own miraculous stories. My sister and I were raised Roman Catholic but we also honour my father's Hindu faith and family deity.

In both Italian and Indian family traditions, single adults remain in their parents' household until marriage and may return after divorce, as I did. It's a more efficient way to pool resources and stay close. There is no shame, whereas in Anglo-Saxon families in the UK or USA, adults living with their parents are deemed failures. Spiralling housing costs in the UK have forced younger people to remain, or return to live, with their parents, causing attitudes to shift. My parents wanted me at home with them. Later, my presence helped when Ma was disabled by a rare neurological disease that slowly tortured and destroyed her.

3. On the Adventures of an Investment Banker:

Ma wasn't happy with the long hours and travel schedule with my work. One day I arrived home from a short trip to Rome or Milan. I stepped out of the taxi and walked in through our front gate. There she was, my mother, standing in the porch twenty feet from me, scowling her disapproval of yet another of my absences. I smiled and pulled out from my flight bag a duty-free box of two hundred cigarettes, waving them as though a flag of surrender and a peace offering. The cigarettes were Ma's favourite Italian brand. The scowl transformed into a bright smile. I was granted most-wonderful-daughter status and welcomed home.

For many years we would look back and laugh together about how her opinions and moods changed according to her self-interest.

I did not realise then how her smoking habit had damaged her health. I never bought her cigarettes again. I would rather risk most-detested-daughter status than enable her addiction.

I inherited my mother's firm but feminine jawline, high forehead and cheekbones, and long wavy hair; from my father, brown almond eyes and full lips. My sister and I grew tall, full-breasted, long-legged, and athletic.

Some men were offended by how a woman's beauty could upset the perceived power balance between men and women. Some men were hostile to the presence of a woman who was their equal at work, who was not there to bolster their egos, who did not seek their approval of her allure, and who would not be intimidated. Most men, I found, were decent and respectful once they realised I was serious in my work: I was neither there to secure career favours by sleeping with influential male colleagues nor hunt for an affluent husband. Women's wealth advisers have a mantra: "A man is not a financial plan."

My tailored suits and red lipstick were my armour while working in a sea of men on the trading floor. I suspect that was the case for my male colleagues, too, with their fine tailoring, cufflinks, and silk Ferragamo ties. I aimed for quiet elegance over fashionable sexiness in my business wardrobe. I never felt safe showing any feminine vulnerability. I had to know what I was doing and felt more confident when I was properly dressed.

I remember taking a black cab to Heathrow to catch a flight to Milan. This was 1994, and I was in my early thirties. A young woman in full business attire was still a rare sight in London. Most young women then dressed for work to attract and please men. I dressed to please myself. Finding the right clothes was difficult. The only decent retailers then were Episode/Susan Woolf or Fenwick of Bond Street. Other retailers classified women's clothing ranges as:

Desperate Trust Fund Bimbo,

High Street Bimbo,

or

Frump.

No thanks.

The cabbie studied me in his rear-view mirror while driving the cab through light traffic out of the city. I felt uneasy and ignored him. Yet another intrusive male gaze, a mild irritant to my morning. The difference between an admiring glance and an angry glare is intent: Does he intend to celebrate the woman, or to demean her? I had a lot on my mind and wanted silence. This was my first trip representing my employer, a London brokerage firm, to visit an important client, an Italian merchant bank. I looked out of the taxi window at the blue sky, at the wisps of cloud, and the spring sunshine bathing the grass verges of the M4. I was lost in thought. Serene.

'Are you a lawyer? You look like a lawyer. I saw the way you move, the way you touch your face.' His voice broke through my meditation.

'No. I'm a money broker. I buy and sell money.' I spoke with cool courtesy. I brokered deals between banks on insurance-type contracts for the foreign exchange market. These contracts were derivatives known as currency options or FX options. It was my first job in London's financial centre known as The City. I did not wish to justify my career history to a complete stranger. I owed him nothing but cab fare.

Later that year I joined Chase Manhattan, an American bank, as a trading assistant on their global FX Options desk, thanks to my friend, Daniel, who recruited me. The traders on that desk were excellent at their job. They knew it but were never complacent. I would assist them by entering trades into the system with an almost obsessive attention to detail: trade date, currency pair, Dollar amount, call or put option, straddle or strangle or risk reversal, strike price, spot price, volatility, premium.

My colleague, Christian, was an intelligent, slightly built young Englishman. He complained that no matter what he wore he looked twelve years old. He said he would look silly if he sported a goatee beard, fashionable then among young men. He always made me smile. Christian was even more obsessive about the details of each trade than I was. One week, according to our manager, Carl, we had entered seven hundred trades into the system with zero errors. We would run risk reports to confirm the expected profit and loss for each trade and for the whole book. And, each day before 3 p.m., we would exercise options that were expiring "in-the-money" that day.

My colleagues and I were at our desks by 7 a.m. just as our Tokyo colleagues, at eight or nine hours ahead of London, were winding down for the day. At noon, London time, our New York colleagues arrived at their desk, 7 a.m. their time. There was always a lull in the markets around that time: New York would be having breakfast while we, in London, had a quick lunch at our desks. The London desk finished work around 5:30 p.m. when the head trader, Jack, handed over the book to his colleague on the New York options desk. They had another four or five hours of their trading day ahead of them.

The guys on the "Quant" desk amazed me. I had never before met people with advanced degrees and even PhDs in Mathematics. A couple of these guys, known as Quantitative Analysts, educated me on the supreme significance of their qualifications as follows:

Bachelor of Science degree, B.S. means "Bull Shit."
Masters degree in Science, M.Sc. means "More Shit."
Doctor of Philosophy, Ph.D. means "Pile it high and Deep."

I lobbied my managers at Chase to send me to an intensive one-week options trading course at INSEAD, an elite business school near Paris. It was a class of a dozen bankers and traders from financial institutions based in Europe. We went deep into the equations and parameters that underpin option pricing and trading. I don't remember much of that course today, but it was highly relevant at the time.

Two memories stand out:

A mid-morning break in the college cafe. I stood at the coffee bar and ordered an espresso from the sleek French barista and waited. I sensed male presences to my left; two male graduate students, crisp American East Coast accents, had arrived at my side. They stood a little too close to me. One spoke to the other.

'You should go for these European women – hot-blooded, dark, mysterious, volatile.'

I was the only woman standing there. Their words were harmless enough, but the lazy tone of their voices jarred within me. They spoke not from their hearts but from their pricks. I felt distinctly uncomfortable. I did not turn to face them. The barista handed me my espresso and I thanked him in French. I pretended to be completely lost in thought and quietly turned away from the two Americans. I joined my classmates and professor who were standing and chatting a few metres away.

When I saw myself through the eyes of those two male graduate students, I was not an attractive, intelligent woman with dreams, ambitions, and desires of my own.

To them, I was simply an exotic variant of college pussy.

The second memory that stands out from that week at INSEAD, was how impressed I was by the teaching faculty, their mastery of the theory of option pricing and trading. I wondered how come they didn't apply their knowledge and trade the markets themselves. They could have made millions of dollars.

I soon realised the skills and qualities required for a successful academic are not the same as those required for a global financial markets trader. The former required a huge ego. The latter, a small ego with the emotional skills and discipline to control their greed and fear.

Trading anything in the global markets, whether cattle, copper, or Swiss Francs, required nerves of steel, an emotional discipline akin to a warrior monk. Any pretensions or testosterone-fuelled bullshit and the markets would kick your backside to the kerb.

Stan was a senior option trader at Chase Manhattan. A burly American who seemed more at home in the beauty of Montana or Wyoming than on a grey London trading floor filled with snarling screens and hissing open telephone lines. He exuded a wisdom and gentleness that charmed me and a searing intelligence that awed everyone. I would have loved to have been his apprentice and run his errands all day long just to glimpse a crumb of his philosophy and discipline.

It was not to be.

Chase Manhattan Bank became the target of an aggressive takeover by Chemical Bank. My boss's boss's boss, usually a jovial Englishman with a legendary tolerance for alcohol, cut short his annual vacation and returned to the floor, ashen-faced. The atmosphere on the trading floor in London became a hotbed of anxiety, uncertainty, and fear. The New York trading floor was even worse.

The options trading team were contractors from a specialist investment firm in Pennsylvania. I was one of their trading assistants but employed by Chase Manhattan Bank. As the takeover by Chemical Bank proceeded, the head trader, Jack, called me into a private meeting.

'You're not learning fast enough,' he said.

'What? But I know I can do this. I just need a little more time.' I was crestfallen.

'I just don't know if you'll ever get it,' he added.

Something in his tone made no sense. His voice, usually resonant, sand and gravel rolling over rocks in the rain, now sounded hollow and flat. I was shocked and hurt. I appreciated the theory and practice of option trading was complex, but I loved it, was hungry to learn, and was always considered capable.

I was being brushed off.

A month or two later Jack pulled me aside and in a rare candid moment said he had a trading assistant in New York who had clerked for him for three years, far too long, but the assistant became a good trader. Jack then said something I will never forget.

'Angela, you would have made a fine trader.'

In 1998, while at HSBC Midland Bank, I noticed BBC Television News cameramen would roam the huge trading floor. They were usually filming an interview with some British politician and used the British bank's trading floor as background. No one paid any attention to them.

I was speaking in Italian over the phone with an important client in Milan. We were finalising the details of an exotic FX option. Unlike a plain vanilla option, an exotic option is a fancy insurance type contract that, in this case, disappeared or "knocked out" if the market price of the underlying currency pair reached a predetermined price known as the trigger. The currency pair was probably Deutschmarks against Italian Lira – the era before the Euro. My mathematician colleagues in the Quant team and the trader in the FX Options team had priced and tailored the exotic option for my client's needs.

When speaking with a client over the phone, I usually stood up to allow my body to move and feel more relaxed in conversation. Thinking on my feet.

We clarified all the details of the deal for my client. My client was about to decide. I suddenly stood straighter, still, my left arm up, bent at the elbow, my forearm held out across my chest to signify to my colleagues that the deal was now in play: the client was about to decide. I shot questions to my colleagues in English and responded to my client in Italian. As soon as the client decided to deal, I lowered my left forearm, my left hand pointed down repeatedly to signify the client had sold us the financial contract as expected. I hung up and wrote up the deal ticket as usual.

The next morning, brokers and other bankers called our desk saying they had seen me on television the night before. BBC news reported the global financial crisis. This was 1998, not 2008.

Little did I know, during that routine deal with my client in Milan, a BBC cameraman was on our trading floor and had quietly filmed me in action. My face was associated with the 1998 global financial crisis caused by a huge hedge fund that had almost gone belly up.

I never saw that news footage.

It did not matter anyway.

Our entire desk got canned a few months later.

When I worked at Citibank, a colleague noticed I was wearing a lovely pashmina shawl in a soft lavender shade. He heard that I hadn't bought it from a luxury store in Knightsbridge but through a mail-order firm at a quarter of the price. He asked me for the mail-order company details – those were the days before online shopping. He later thanked me as his wife was very happy with both her new shawl and her husband.

Sometimes I wore the lavender shawl over an Italian pale-grey trouser suit to counter the cold air-conditioning. Some days the few women on the trading floor would show up for work wearing the same colours. An attractive young blonde at an adjacent desk at Citi showed up one morning, also wearing a pale-grey trouser suit and a long scarf in a lavender shade. We looked at each other up and down and laughed. The men of both desks noticed, were perplexed, and they laughed too. Perhaps our moods had synchronised the day before, influencing our dress colour choices that morning.

I can only guess.

In 1999 President Clinton repealed the Glass-Steagall Act. It was enacted in 1933 as part of banking reforms following the economic crash of 1929. The Glass-Steagall act protected ordinary depositors' money in commercial banks from being gambled away in high-risk ventures typical of investment banks. With that protection now gone, I decided it was time to quit the game. My clients at Citi were throwing their money away in trades without a stop-loss order in place. They were not trading. They were gambling, despite my efforts to advise them otherwise. The global financial markets had been my career home for six years. It was time to leave this global casino.

In June 2000 I spent a weekend at a personal development course in Stockholm, Sweden. I had an epiphany:

I am a writer, not a banker.

On Monday morning, I gave notice to my boss, a firm but fair English gentleman Citibanker. He smiled and understood. By then, I was no longer working on the trading floor but as a risk analyst upstairs.

The repeal of the Glass-Steagall Act gave big banks room to get even bigger, borrowing even more against the depositor accounts now included in their global capital. The economic meltdown of 2008 only surprised me because it had not happened sooner.

33

THE POWER OF WITNESS

~ Clara ~

I am no longer afraid to meet Xoran again. He is James in this life and will not remember me. Little does he know, one day he, too, will become a statue, a headless but exquisite marble form. A wealthy financier will acquire Xoran's statue at an obscure art auction. Within a few years the financier will experience inexplicable losses of his considerable wealth and wellbeing. He will donate the statue to the gardens of a thriving church in Santa Clara County. He will jump to his death from the forty-eighth floor of a building in San Francisco's Financial District.

The church will fall into decay within a few years of the headless statue's arrival. The once vibrant congregation, beset with scandal, will suffer a bitter dissolution. The immaculate gardens and cemetery will become dark, dank, and disused.

The passing of time will bring the widening of the nearby freeway. Commercial pressures on government to repeal laws protecting sacred land will allow rapid development of a shopping mall and apartment complex desecrating the cemetery and church land. Xoran's statue will be moved out of the cemetery to whereabouts unknown.

Evil has neither a face nor a location but it does exist. Evil is strengthened by doubt, confusion, and fear. It is weakened by light, truth, and justice. I could be swept away in fear and confusion, sowing doubt and weakening my resolve. I have seen this game played too often over the millennia by government officials like James. They create a powerful vortex of fear to control their people and subdue dissent. They lead their people to believe no alternative way exists but to obey without question. I refuse to believe this lie. I choose instead to follow that still quiet voice of wisdom within me. I choose to seek justice, bring light, and unveil the true story.

To stand apart and transcend fear takes courage. When I was alive, I lost that strength of heart. I could not think for myself. I did not trust that feeling in my body when something did not feel true.

I am a restless statue. My thirst for learning became an addiction. I feared I had missed something important in all my endless analyses. All the analyses and logic in the world could never satisfy my craving during my transition to a new paradigm of being. My impossible desire for control caused my addiction. Little did I know, my heart was the only infallible guide through the confusion and darkness.

It was necessary to lose my mind to find my heart. My mind had become rigid. It could not tolerate things it did not know and imprisoned my heart behind walls of fear.

The fear fades in the light of new consciousness and compassion. Old beliefs in pain and suffering once hidden in my body now melt away. They no longer dictate my choices with anonymity. They no longer exert power and influence without accountability. My choices and decisions are no longer made from fear. My will is now free. My choices are now made from love.

34

I Don't Know

~ Eleanor ~

Dark moods consumed me. What is the point of living if this is all there is? I could not find any pleasure in the simplest of things. Everything was an effort. My heart felt numb. Life was joyless.

I was seated at my usual spot, on the curved marble bench to Clara's left. The bench had not yet cast a shadow near her plinth. The stone had a sparkle today. Maybe it was just the angle of the afternoon sun.

'Acknowledge the emotions no matter how heavy they are. Breathe and release them. Do not get trapped in the drama behind them,' Clara said. Her voice resounded in my heart. 'In this way they bring peace and transformation to your being. Your emotions are signals from the soul that craves resolution and growth. You are here to evolve.'

'If I had known the pain and heartache, I would never have fallen in love. But then I would never have come to San Francisco.' I said.

'And you would not have experienced the spiritual awakening that brought you here today. Be with the mystery. Not all knowledge may be revealed when desired. Knowledge revealed too soon may be misinterpreted and frighten an evolving consciousness.' Clara said.

'Why is it so hard? I panic when I don't know what I'm doing next.' I said.

'If you listen only to your rational mind for guidance and do not also engage your heart then, of course, every step you take becomes stifled by endless analyses. Your life proceeds according to the dictates of fear.'

'How do I engage my heart?'

'Listen and honour your feelings and emotions. You do not allow yourself to be ruled by them. For example, on one particular day you may have angry feelings that have no connection to a circumstance or event outside of yourself. The anger has no apparent cause. Acknowledge and accept that on that particular day you have angry feelings. It does not mean you are an angry person. It does not mean that you resolve the anger by taking violent action against yourself or another person. The anger may be masking a deeper emotion like sadness. You may be releasing old subconscious beliefs that no longer serve you. Your old beliefs or persistent thought patterns may be fading away. Give space to the emotions. Witness them without judgement. You may soon feel ideas and inspiration bubbling up from your heart that could lead you to greater joy, your birthright.'

'It's hard to acknowledge emotions when they are in full flow through me. It's hard to be so detached.'

'You are not detached. You choose to be the calm centre, the eye of the storm. Remember, emotions ebb and flow. You have the wisdom to know they are not permanent. Practise this wisdom: be still and observe the nature of the emotions. Where do they arise in your body? Where in your body do you feel tension or pain?'

'I can feel them in my body?'

'Yes, with practice. In this post-industrial civilisation, time for daily reflection and contemplation is essential for mental, emotional, physical, and above all, spiritual health. The average person sees this time as an indulgence, a luxury, while the most influential and powerful will not let a day pass without examining their motives, thoughts, and relationships. The courage to act on their intuitive ideas is the secret to their wealth. The discipline to take time each day for quiet thought is the secret to their influence. The clarity of thought that arises is the secret to their power. This power may be misused to control and suppress or even destroy the lives of others for their own gain. However, those of higher consciousness will use their power and influence for the benefit of the entire planet.'

'What about love, Clara? Seems an empty world with only power, influence, and wealth.'

'A wise thought, Eleanor. Those who seek power and wealth for their personal gain will attract those with similar motives. It is a divine mercy that they will not realise the emptiness of their lives. Their limited consciousness will see relationships as a tacit agreement to exploit each other for as long as each person fulfils the expectations of the other. Infatuation soon becomes boredom and indifference.'

'There must be more to life than that. No wonder you see so many living statues.'

'It is my greatest sadness to observe so many who live in defeat, their dreams dead, but I have seen many who inspire me. Those who live from the heart. Their consciousness is focused on following their passion and bringing joy to the world. They may be lawyers, bankers, artists, janitors, homemakers, business owners, but their hearts are in what they do. When you love your work, you cannot help but transform the world around you.'

'My life has been a waste of time. I seem to lurch from one mess to another, breaking my heart to pieces. I confused love with lust. It was only sex, only blind ambition. All ego.'

'To grow, it is sometimes necessary to break open your heart. Breathe through the pain and face it. Feel it in your body and it will lessen. Imagine your pain dedicated to alleviating the suffering of others in far worse circumstances around the world. Your romantic and career adventures have taught you far more than you realise. Each soulmate, each career step, though temporary, has been an invaluable teacher.'

'I thought a soulmate was forever.'

'Not always. Some souls cross our path for a short time, but the experience opens us to new ideas and perspectives that would not have been possible before their encounter.'

'I am tired of this obsession with romantic relationships. I want to be like you, Clara. You are so self-contained and free of all that crap.'

'To love is to live. I grieve still for the loss of my love, Richard. For millennia he has searched for me in many incarnations. His efforts were doomed to failure until he lived as an English sculptor called Marcus in Italy over a century ago. Richard saw my spirit as an apparition trapped in that block of marble. He hewed away at the marble with love to reveal my present form.'

'What was it like to see him again?'

'A bittersweet longing. His heart was broken. He had been betrayed by an heiress who resembled me in a superficial way. My heart ached for him, for just as they had planned to declare their love publicly, her engagement to another suitor, a wealthy aristocrat, was announced and she left for London without a word to him. Working on my form in that cave in Italy healed him. He even felt compassion for the difficulties his beloved had in confronting the strictures of her family and class. Her love for him was too feeble in its fantasy to survive beyond a summer romance. She never meant him harm but the heiress, self-absorbed as usual, never knew the depth of his love for the woman he thought she was.'

'He was in love with a fantasy? He was infatuated?'

'Not quite. Richard, as Marcus, was in love with the heiress because in her quiet independence, privilege, and nobility, he mistook her for me.'

'Something about her had triggered past-life memories of his love for you?'

'That is the danger of falling in love in haste. An image or a memory deep in your subconscious may have been awakened. Take time to acquaint yourself with the actual person present otherwise, in your enthusiasm, you could be mistaken.'

'Is that what I did in my last relationship?'

'That may be, but do not invalidate neither the experience nor your beloved, for they were in accordance with divine will. Without him, your heart would not be broken open today. You would not have cleared away the illusion of who you thought you were. You would not have heard my voice. I only speak into the hearts of those whose hearts are open.'

'I am learning to be grateful even for the unhappy events in my life.' I said.

'With gratitude comes strength and resilience of purpose because your attention turns to matters of higher energy: your destiny may then be revealed. Your body becomes light.'

'All this from gratitude?'

'It is impossible to fathom the importance of this one quality in life. Without gratitude, no matter how rich you are in material possessions, you will be poor in spirit, and therefore, in wealth. The most powerful of prayers is, "Thank you" because of the expansion of consciousness that accompanies the words said with a pure heart.'

'Clara, I am ashamed to admit that I'm angry at my past. I can't handle the present. I'm scared of a future that I cannot see.'

'Eleanor, your anger is not the indignant indulgence of a little girl. Your anger is profound and legitimate. You live in an age that does not honour feminine intelligence and wisdom but seeks instead to suppress and denigrate your gifts. To be feminine is seen as weak by a masculine culture degraded by threat of brute force. Opportunities to create true wealth for all are wasted in the pursuit of self-interests. To survive, women today are encouraged to behave like men in their careers and with their families. Women expect to achieve all the fiction they were taught to believe. The reality of too many conflicting responsibilities falls far short of the dream. They blame themselves for being inadequate while forsaking their own needs like rest and play. However, the anger arising in women is the intuitive realisation they have been misled. While their economic freedoms are greater, their workload has more than doubled. Living costs have risen faster than salaries. A family now needs two breadwinners. To raise children without her own income is now a luxury few women can afford.'

The shadows had lengthened across Clara's plinth. We fell into our customary silence that I always found so rich and nourishing. The afternoon breeze felt cool. I wrapped my cotton scarf around my shoulders. It was time to leave.

'Thank you, Clara.' A warm glow radiated from my heart. 'I'll be back.'

35

ANGER

~ Eleanor ~

Through the dark storms of anger in my forties I found, at last, a small measure of peace: I embraced my destiny. I stopped obsessing about ever meeting the right man. It seems in our present culture that a mature divorced woman must be lonely and frustrated. She must be a failure in life if she is not part of a couple. Or, even worse, there must be something wrong with her feminine character.

Enough.

In a few years, I will be fifty years old. It has taken me discipline and spirit to overcome the many disempowering themes in a toxic, youth-obsessed culture. Lies permeate broadcast media that all persons over a certain age, except the very rich and powerful, are of no value, are irrelevant, are unhealthy, have memory problems, have less energy, are no longer vital or sexy.

For a year or two, I believed these lies and stopped taking regular exercise and watching my diet. What was the point in these precautions if my decline was inevitable? My health suffered as a consequence and I fell into the trap of thinking the cause was my age. Upon deeper reflection, I could see I had neglected my body's fundamental need for joyful movement and nutrition.

My short-term memory was challenged with more schedules to consider other than my own, more on my mind with increasing responsibilities. Grief caused lapses in focus as more friends and family members died. Funerals became regular events, with no more weddings, and no christenings.

I could see younger people wasting their energies chasing illusory goals in the hope of happiness and success. Instead, they would become embittered and burnt out by long working hours and a relentless pace with abusive corporate employers. Older people are more discerning and less likely to fall for false inducements.

Ageing became an adventure once I learned how to protect my mental, physical, emotional, and spiritual health.

In my younger days, I worked in financial markets littered with men who were taught to dishonour and disrespect women and girls as weak and stupid. The western world normalises images of half-naked women across its media. Those who dare to question this dishonour are ridiculed and accused of being neurotic or "crazy".

A woman who can take care of her own material and emotional needs may be more selective in who she takes as a mate. This power terrifies the mediocre man. Far easier to deny a woman an education and fair-paid work, cut her genitals, rape her, and beat her than face the path of the true heroic masculine: to serve and protect the feminine.

When a women's intelligence is suppressed, the whole planet suffers: more of the mediocre masculine and manipulative feminine procreate, steeped in greed and fear, preventing intelligent stewardship of our planet. Corruption weakens countries that remain poor despite abundant resources.

This world aches for heroes and human goddesses to inspire a new generation of humanity. Together they can heal our planet. Heroes are men of wisdom, strength, and honour. Human goddesses are women who are complete in themselves. They define themselves by their mission and passion. They are visionary. They are kind. They are compassionate. They are lethal to the mediocre man.

I feel sorry for the mediocre man. He sees only with his eyes. He hears only with his ears. His only pleasures are through his stomach and penis. Life may be felt through the heart in all its richness and glory, but this miracle is denied him until his shrivelled heart gives way to disease and death.

A man without a decent heart is like a warrior without strength. He can be manipulated by societal pressures and used until he is useless and then discarded. Are men angry too? Are they angry at a system they created and perpetuate by their silence and compliance? Men are victims, too, even if society was designed for their needs. They comply to survive. Societal systems like racism, sexism, socio-economic classes, and other forced inequalities are kept in place by an unaccountable elite to maintain their power and influence to divide and rule. Accepting the way things are without question betrays a mind accustomed to and enslaved by outside influence. An enslaved consciousness can be liberated by the right questions.

Emotional independence for a woman is as essential as economic independence. Many women in western civilisation seem so desperate to be in a romantic relationship with a man. I wish they would wake up and learn to be in a healthy relationship with themselves first. Without honour and love for myself, no healthy relationship with another can survive but becomes an endless co-dependency with, and control by, a mediocre man.

Clara taught me to take personal responsibility for everything in my life. I would have found that impossible when I believed I was the victim of some unhappy circumstance. Blaming myself, others, and everything for my misery imprisoned me in my own hell. Blame, guilt, and shame were the secure locks on that heavy door to my freedom.

Being grateful for even the most mundane aspects of my life weakened and broke the locks. Gratitude released creative resources in my mind and heart. I could see with love and compassion where and how I had unwittingly caused my unhappy circumstances.

How could I create heaven on earth?

By taking great care over every detail in life.

When I am careless, the devil is in the detail, where my assumptions are the mother of all my mishaps. On those rare occasions when I am a genius, the divine is in the fine detail, the twists and turns of thought not discernible to my usually coarse mind.

Where there is great responsibility, there is great power.

Heaven never condemned me.

I created my own hell.

My soul has cried for help for decades. I believed my prayers were ignored. I felt unworthy to have my prayers answered. My bitterness grew in strength, a silent assassin further poisoning my faith. Depression and anxiety, my constant companions, sucked energy from any idea, any thought that would have allowed respite and freedom.

I learned from Clara that my prayers were made without faith, without expectation they would be answered. I prayed as though to a vile, capricious god. In my unconscious mind I prayed for my prayers go unanswered to fulfil the unfolding drama of "poor me, nothing I do makes any difference".

I learned that my prayers were sincere but I failed to heed the guidance that came through my intuition. I did not listen to the faint, still voice in my heart. My anger swamped my courage to act on intuition. I needed logical cause to satisfy my ego before risking the next step. And I wondered why my actions made no difference. The actions I took were fruitless. My prayers were answered every time. I was too stubborn, or too stupid, to listen.

Clara's voice saved me. Her gentleness born of strength, majesty, and compassion opened my heart and I surrendered.

I now see the purpose of my darkness: to show me the way to the divine through my own dark heart. Just as when the student is ready the master appears, so it is when the darkness is ready, the light appears.

36

WARRIOR OF THOUGHT

~ Memoir ~ Author ~

Clara is my immortal teacher, a voice in my heart from another dimension of space and time. I wish I could see her in my dreams. I wish I could hear her voice with more clarity. Usually, I don't hear anything. It's more an urgent feeling in the heart I need to articulate and write down with a clear, focused mind.

For me, writing is a spiritual practice. Writing is hard work but I always feel happier and more alive when I've completed a session, even if I didn't quite know what I was doing.

My spiritual training may not be advanced enough to handle a direct meeting with an ascended master like Clara. At times, I feel her close by, especially when I am still and peaceful. I discovered a richness in my solitude as a writer: a warrior of thought – someone who can construct their own narrative. I even started a daily meditation practice to strengthen the stillness and become a warrior of peace – someone who feels emotions flow through their body but remains unswayed by any drama from judgement, fear, or upset.

A warrior of thought sees through the fallacies, the illusory arguments of the ignorant, the manipulative, and the deceitful. A warrior of thought may be a poet whose words express a truth so powerful that a nation is liberated from the lies of a corrupt government. A warrior of thought may be a spiritual master, a mortal trained in stillness of thought. Mental and spiritual training is training for mortal combat.

How do I stop the mind from thinking? A warrior of thought knows. A spiritual adept knows. A poet knows. They all practise some form of meditation. They don't stop the thoughts, but they stop attaching any emotion and feeling to them. They observe any thoughts that may arise and let them fade away. They practise the power of being present without the clutter of thoughts in a state of intense clarity, focus, and concentration. Athletes call this state, being "in the zone" because they, too, are warriors of thought. They slay the demons of doubt and fear to transcend limits of human achievement.

Writing a book is like a battle. The innocent writer charges forward with clear plans and strategies proven from the annals of ancient military history. The theatre of war will bring to light and challenge all the writer's assumptions. So, I thought it would be easy to take that ridge defending my delusions? To invade and destroy that country of my blissful ignorance? I thought it would be easy to write a chapter a week? A book in three months?

How arrogant I was.

Some would rather die than own up to their foolishness and make the appropriate changes to their strategy. And many do: soldiers die in battle when their commanders underestimate their enemy and miscalculate battle conditions; writers kill themselves in the face of doubts, fears, and the many lies unmasked, revealing who they truly are.

I scraped together all the courage I could and more to face the abyss of my own humanity and return with a smile of compassion. I now know why most people who say they'd love to write a book, never do. Compassion saved my life. In the dark hours of writing this book, the pain of constant failure to ever make any difference in life, the mounting debts, the loneliness, the failure to make any comprehensible progress with the book, almost proved too much to bear. My ego could not stand the hell of not knowing what I was doing.

If I had taken my own life, I know my friends and family would have suffered. Instead, I wrote myself a stay of execution: I wrote a little every day.

And help came.

I have much to be grateful for in life even if this book remains unread by another soul.

There is a saying, "When you are going through hell, keep going." The repetitive and useless nature of my existence created an illusory hell. There seemed to be no point to and no progress in my work and wellbeing. I seemed to get fatter and poorer. My efforts seemed endless with no tangible results. I felt as though I was going insane because I was doing the same things every day but getting nowhere.

For a few years, I resisted my writing duties every day because I feared the searing clarity on the page. A truth once written could only transform the writer. I feared I would become destitute if I surrendered to the artist's way. I was scared to let go of who I thought I should have been, a successful employee or some fantasy corporate titan. I knew that was not my path, but I had no stable sense of who I was anymore. The banker in me was never going to fall for the starving artist archetype. I felt vulnerable without a career, without a husband, without a reliable income, without a sense of belonging. I lived with my parents and sister but I didn't feel safe. The extent of my self-judgement and condemnation for my perceived failures crippled my courage to open up, let go, and have faith in my imminent transformation.

But help came.

Healing began when my sister introduced me to a network spinal analysis (NSA) chiropractor in the summer of 2006. I saw how my sister had become more relaxed and joyful after just a few sessions. I became more open-minded and open-hearted. Past traumas were released over time. This was no overnight miracle. Instead, I opened up to the miracle of writing down what I felt in my heart from Clara and felt more at peace in my body. In one entrainment session, lying face down on a massage-type bench, I felt heavy armour plates over my shoulder blades separate from my spine and fall away to the floor. This was energetic armour that had hidden my true self and had crushed any possibility of joy.

In another NSA entrainment session, I felt so relaxed, I slipped into a blissful blackness. I am not one to faint or pass out without cause. Did I go to another dimension? I don't know. I remember Dr Suzette, my chiropractor, speaking out loud into my right ear.

'Angela, come back.'

I felt cold. My body was immobile. I was aware of the chiropractor's office and my body's weight on the bench. I was a flowing mass of translucent energy. A slow and sedate tide trickled back into my body, an earthly suit of armour where my arms were its sleeves. My hands were its gloves. The energies flowed into my fingertips. I was back.

'You had stopped breathing,' Dr Suzette said. She was calm. There was no cause for alarm.

I had left my body. I could have happily floated away had Dr Suzette not called me back. It wasn't my time. I still had more work to do.

In the autumn of 2006, I had my first session with Wesley, a spiritual coach and a friend. We had met at a Landmark Education course in San Francisco two years earlier. We worked together by telephone regularly until 2020. At the time of writing, we still speak a few times a year. He seems to know when I need assistance and calls me out of the blue.

In spring 2009, Wesley recommended I have a few Vortex Healing sessions. They cleared away very heavy energies of grief and sadness in my body that prevented me finishing an early draft of this book. Daisy, my Vortex Healer, counselled me that I would be able to finish this book once I fully loved myself. At the time, I did not understand what Daisy was talking about. Over the years since, with greater wisdom and humility, I can now see how right she was. I had no idea how hard on myself I was, how I had strangled my own creative expression.

One by one over the years, the limiting beliefs that held my spirit hostage were dissolved in the light. Without guidance from Clara, without expert help in learning to listen to and trust my intuition, my awakening would not have been possible. I had come close to suicide a few times with the bouts of depression that used to engulf me. I was never clinically diagnosed because the depression only ever lasted a day or two. I was lucky they didn't last weeks or months. I would not have survived.

Eventually in 2015–2016, I made decisions that seemed to make no sense at the time, like changing my diet and embarking on intense training in Angelic Reiki. Looking back now, those decisions made perfect sense.

I followed my heart despite the many protests from my mind, like: 'Are you mad?'

'You're already vegetarian and you're fine.'

'Going vegan is extreme. It's stupid. You'll die.'

'Your Italian and Indian families consume dairy, eggs, and honey. You're betraying your heritage.'

'That reiki course costs a lot of money. Are you sure you know what you are doing?'

The dramas were only in my head. None of the above protests from my mind proved to be true. My heart was right all along.

The journey from my head to my heart has not been for my benefit alone. Being happier and peaceful is the best gift I could ever give another.

37

AWAKENING

~ Clara ~

Of all my horses, I miss Andromeda the most. On a clear, crisp day with the sun behind us, she could spring into an effortless gallop. I would feel alive, so light and free as though we flew through the sky.

Why the cold ache through my soul?

Richard.

He would always ride alongside me. His mare, as fine and as black as Andromeda, had twin white star markings on her forehead compared to Andromeda's single star. Today, at times, I see those stars in the sky. The merest reminder of Richard floods my body with cold needles of pain: the soft sandalwood and citrus aroma in his hair, the dry muskiness of his scent after a long ride, his quiet poise and gentleness borne of strength and intelligence. Above all, I remember the golden smile in his eyes whenever he saw me.

The pain is deep. I cannot bear to feel it any longer.

Was this love but a distant dream?

Marble keeps memories and their intense emotions locked in its crystalline structure. The locks are too secure for my comfort. The memories have not faded over time but have burned into my soul.

There is nowhere to hide from the power of such a love, nowhere on earth, not in heaven, or even in hell. He will find me again, if not in this lifetime then certainly the next. My foolish ignorance cost him his life. He fell victim to treachery at my court.

'There was nothing to forgive,' the angel said. 'He would have died a thousand times for you, without question.'

'Could such a love have existed? Was it true?' My statue mind invented many ways to deny the memories to numb and refute the pain, all to no avail. The heaviness in my heart silenced my thoughts. 'I am not worthy of such a love again.' A fine glow of anger reverberated in my heart, lifting heavy shadows of doubt and confusion.

'Only a statue could have so little faith,' he smiled. His light faded from view but his presence, as always, remained.

The angel once said anger is the first sign of an awakening heart. That was probably five thousand years ago. I do not remember. I do remember I did not believe him then. I had only ever known my murderous anger and icy rage. Maybe now I may comprehend his words through the new wisdom of my heart instead of my rational mind. Anger may cleanse the heart by burning bright. This anger of awakening is not my corrosive resentment that destroyed me and many innocent souls. The anger of awakening may burn away the lie and reveal the true essence of who I am:

Love.

38

Pressure

~ Clara ~

The sun has set. I may only imagine the crimson haze left by the sinking star on the horizon behind me. My plinth was installed to face east. The first stars are visible in the deepening sky. I do not see their constellations, only their distant, lonely beauty. I remember the cold brilliance, the fire, and the scintillation of the diamonds that once adorned my regalia.

A diamond is formed deep in the mantle of the earth by intense heat and pressure on molten carbon.

Marble is formed by intense heat and pressure on limestone.

Heat, pressure, and aeons of time.

Rough crystalline rocks can be cut with expert care into exquisite gems.

I had many jewels set with rare gems. Diamonds of many colours, rubies, and sapphires were of particular favour. They are lost to time, scattered by the civilisations succeeding Xoran's reign over my former realm. Some possessions marked me as a descendant of an august lineage. My swords, my jewels, were some examples. My horses' livery and those of my personal guards were other examples that signalled my presence to those who did not otherwise recognise me.

Who I am truly has little to do with material possessions. They were only symbols of continuity bequeathed to me by my ancestors, representing my high office. Little did I know, I would fail. Little did I know the disaster I would cause. I could live in peace if the failure affected me alone. How do I forgive myself when I feel the weight of all those who died bearing down on my soul?

'They were not lost,' the angel said. 'Their souls were gathered soon after death by my fellow angels entrusted with this special mission.'

I did not understand my heavenly companion. What did he mean by special mission? I knew he could see my thoughts.

'During war, when many thousands of souls are passing together from human to spirit form, my fellow angels, powerful soul gatherers, descend onto the battlefields and collect each soul into safety. Wounded soldiers may see a strange glow in the sky as they hover between life and death.'

'Are you not a soul-gatherer angel too?'

'Yes, Clara, but my mission is to gather and accompany your soul alone.'

My heavenly companion could silence me with the power of love emanating from every wave and every particle of his being. As usual, the trees quivered in delight whenever he appeared by my side, especially when he submerged his being into the ground, his eyes level with mine, and his throat at ground level. I felt the earth beneath my plinth tremble with healing energy.

I never thought to ask his name.

And then one day, he said, 'My name is Michael.'

39

THE DANCE OF CREATIVITY

~ Memoir ~ Author ~

I have always been a detailed, precise, and conscientious person. But would I say I was a creative person? I'd say no.

Hell no.

What would Clara say?

What would she have me say here? My ego gets in the way, that's all. The ego is not a bad thing. It's a part of me that wants to feel safe in familiar ways of living. I would not grow and achieve anything if I stuck to the familiar ways. If I want my life to change, I have to change the things in my life that no longer serve me.

I was scared of writing. Yet, I love Clara and was obsessed with writing her story. For years I struggled with little progress in my writing, and therefore, in my life.

I had to change my attitudes.

Was I going to follow my love or my fear?

I believed I had to be happy and calm before I started working on the book. I believed I had to know what I was doing, that I had a clear plan. Any anxiety meant I was doing something wrong and that I was not capable of writing the book, that it was beyond me. It was only when I heard successful authors speak that I finally realised I had it all wrong. Of course I do not know what I am doing. I am not supposed to know. The initial phases of putting a book together is an exploration. The middle phases are a mystery. The final phases? I do not know yet. So far, it seems to be a discovery. I had little idea what this book was about until my editor read an earlier draft. Her feedback helped me see the book in a new light. I once heard Oprah Winfrey say in an interview about her strategy that she simply does "the next right thing".

I learned to follow my heart and show up.

I made changes to my daily habits.

On waking in the morning, I write for about ten minutes. Sometimes more, sometimes less. I use a favourite cheap rollerball pen and loose leaf lined paper which I keep by my bedside. I later discard the paper. I dump all my concerns, anxieties, any dreams or nightmares, any fears that bubbled up through my consciousness overnight. It's like "taking out the trash" as my American friends would say – daily mental cleansing. I am grateful to Julia Cameron for her book, *The Artist's Way* – for this tip which I spent many years resisting. I was either an idiot or I wasn't yet ready to handle the consequences. Finally, hearing an online marketing expert, Seth Godin, speak of his book, *The Practice*, about producing creative work, convinced me to start my morning journal. I was ready at last to implement this powerful practice. Thank you, Julia Cameron. Thank you, Seth Godin.

Writer's block for me is fear and resistance. I found discipline to be the best weapon: show up and do the work even if it's not my best that day. Get it done. Stephen Pressfield's book, *The War of Art*, destroyed writer's block for me forever. When I surrendered to fear and indecision, my mental health suffered. Mr Pressfield gives vivid examples in his book of how an artist's life can go haywire if they do not follow their calling. I had never seen or heard it expressed this way before. That was the end of writer's block for me. I found the more I trusted my intuition, the less blocked I felt in my writing.

Meditation is a daily essential practice for me, a habit I have stuck to. Or rather, it's a habit that sticks to me. Twenty to thirty minutes or more before the morning journal clears the static electricity from, and refreshes, my brain. I become productive and calm. On rare days that I do not meditate, my focus is scattered, and I am almost dyspraxic in my movements. I have energy but fail to use it properly, like the wheels of a vehicle spinning in soft sand. The familiar weariness of depression then looms. A pall of gloom descends over everything.

Five or six days per week, I practise yoga for a few minutes morning and evening according to my body's needs. I find a short regular practice prevents stiffness and injury, leaving me free to move with ease despite my mature age. It feels good, too, and helps my focus and concentration. The more fluid my body feels, the easier and stronger my intuition and creative mind.

I spend a few minutes before bedtime writing my evening journal. I use an elegant silver pen exclusively for this practice and a journal of exquisite design. I record any notable events that day and anything I could be grateful for. This kept me sane when my mother was tortured and destroyed by a slow, incurable disease. I write down any questions I need answers to but am at a loss to answer myself. A trick I learned from Julia Cameron as well as author, Marie Forleo: write the question and keep my hand moving across the page with the pen. The answer usually comes down through the moving pen onto the page. It seems my body, or my subconscious mind, knows the answer and responds to the question posed by my conscious mind.

Julia Cameron once wrote, "writing rights your life". Anything that has been bothering me deep down comes up in my journal and I deal with it, eventually. Sometimes that can be a struggle: I was scared to drop the extra twenty pounds or ten kilos in weight I was carrying. It no longer served me to feel so heavy. I had gained weight after my mother's death. My psychological boundaries had been blown in the emotional earthquake after losing Ma. The extra bulk on my body had given me the illusion of safety and security, a bigger physical boundary where I could hide my broken heart. Once I realised I could feel happier in my body and was psychologically secure, I no longer needed the extra physical weight. I released the twenty pounds over a six-month period with professional guidance.

I struggled to let go of the old comfortable habits, who I used to be, and embrace the unknown, the person I was becoming.

The struggle is part of the writing faith, part of the artist's way.

Clara says patience is the ability to trust in the perfect unfolding of it all. She advises me to be still and be at peace for all is coming through in its own time. The dreams that become reality are the ones I believe in, where I stand firm no matter what the external circumstances. Compromising my dreams just because they seem impossible may soothe my scared ego but will displease my higher self.

Clara warned me that following through on any dream risks encountering my inner voices of self-doubt, confusion, and self-loathing. I called these voices My Furies after the goddesses of vengeance and retribution in Greek mythology. The only crime I had committed was to be alive and dare to dream. My Furies challenged my sanity, but all the lies I had once held dear were dispelled. One of those lies was that I need to work hard and earn lots of money to deserve love. As a writer, I earned no money at all but I pursued my dream of writing and publishing this book. I earned a little money working part time in a wonderful small business in London as an administrative assistant. There, I learned to honour myself and manage the money I had with power and responsibility. I learned it was never the amount of money that was important but how I managed what I had. These frugal habits have served me well in distinguishing price versus value – a common misconception that divides the poor from the rich.

My deepest desire is to bring Clara's story to the world. Her voice will be known and heard. People will be inspired and empowered by who she is and the ancient wisdom she brings to the modern world.

Clara says desire is the beginning of any creative act.

She advised me to walk through the darkness alone and new friends will appear. They will appear when I am true to myself. Listen out for them because they may be obscured at first by My Furies who may sabotage the journey. My Furies will be at their darkest just before I break through to a new dawn of being. My Furies are not my enemy, Clara says, they are my teachers. To conquer and defuse their lethal force, simply embrace them because they are part of my humanity. The only danger is in believing what they say:

'You're stupid.'

'You're a complete failure.'

'Who in their right mind would read this crap?'

'Why are you wasting time writing this useless book? Get a real job.'

And my favourite:

'Nothing you do makes any damned difference.'

My Furies went quiet when I stopped worrying about who I was anymore and instead focused on getting the work done from my heart, not my ego.

The heroine's journey?

Perhaps.

A woman's quest for sanity and inner peace in a world of corrupted masculine values: work so hard that I destroy my health enslaved to the illusion of a happier future in a system rigged to keep most people in poverty while competing against others to diminish them. I prefer to compete with others, to exalt them and test for weaknesses in my own game.

I trust I will clearly see the next step to take in life. Even if I feel fear and discomfort, I trust that my higher self has already taken everything into account.

This week, I am at peace with the ebb and flow of writing. I am at peace with the interruptions and I keep going. The ebb and flow of writing is a rhythm that becomes a tyrant only when I hang on to my past emotional pain; only when I resist the natural flow. The rhythm of writing cleanses that crap out of my life. If each day I practise clarity and focus, I become strong, resilient, and playful.

The book gets done.

The trick is to enjoy the journey.

40

A STRANGE ENERGY

~ Clara ~

Sunshine strengthens my meditation at sunrise and sunset. The nights are my retreat but for the moon. Her light, so cold, so severe, disturbs the serenity of my stone form awakening ancient memories. Deep within me stirs the white heat of anger then the cooling ache of infinite sadness. Some emotions refuse to settle. Some refuse to be forgotten.

I no longer fight them. Fighting makes the pain worse. Instead, I stand firm in the storm of emotions raging through me, keeping my heart soft. The storm subsides by sunrise.

The angel always instructs me to stand firm with a soft and open heart. At first, I did not believe him. It seemed an impossible feat. How on earth could I achieve such a formidable strength of heart and mind?

That, the angel reminds me, is the purpose of my meditation at sunrise and sunset.

My destiny was to "live" in the northern latitudes of this beautiful planet. I am a witness. One act of violence at the wrong time and place may beget war. A wise ruler knows that to commit her armed forces to war in anger may lead to loss of life and the total destruction of a civilisation. The spiritual masters, the fine generals, artists, scholars, merchants, and artisans are the riches of any civilisation. A millennium may pass before lost arts and marvels of engineering are rediscovered. Most are lost forever. Some empires thrive and endure while others wither to oblivion.

My empire withered to oblivion. There remains no trace of my past. Today, I see those I had wronged in their past lifetimes now reborn as glorious human beings. I will help them today.

Aurora watches me with the careful attention of an eagle in her full majesty. Whether she is perched on a branch nearby or hovering a thousand feet above me, I feel the ferocity of her loving presence. Love is not always comfortable: ferocity and tenderness, passion and steadfastness may exist side by side.

The strange energy I feel is that kind of love, untainted by any requirement to alter or hide my true self. It is pure. It accepts me and my shame. I am only required to accept this love, allow it to enter my heart, and open up to a new world of grace. The world will not grow and transcend its beliefs in the power of fear unless I accept and believe in the power of love. This is the sacred path of the warrior of light. A war fought within me where each battle I face with a strong and open heart.

In each battle, I vanquish my shadows with love.

For so long, I have lived in a harsh and ugly world driven by the survival of the fittest.

A beautiful new world is coming, blessed by the thriving of the kindest.

So be it.

Let the transcendence begin.

41

My Dark Nights

~ Eleanor ~

I am scared. Could I be irreversibly damaged by my past failures in relationships? The urge to protect my heart runs deep. I never trusted myself – a legacy of emotional abuse in childhood; I was too frightened to argue my case with a parent for fear of reprisal. The break in trust began with the first slap across my face. I would go to school with welts on my cheek where my mother's powerful painted nails caught my flesh in the wake of the blow.

I am not angry at my parents anymore. I am now grown. They did the best they could as parents. They just wanted to keep their children safe in, what seemed to them, a terrifying world. Each parent had been traumatised by growing up in a war zone. My father will readily tell stories of his escape unharmed from an ambush by an armed gang in a civil war that left seven of his friends dead and dozens seriously injured. My mother had many stories of a pyrrhic battle in Italy from World War II that she took to her grave. In rare moments of peace and reflection, she would reveal a story as though it had taken place a few weeks, not decades, before. The untold stories hung around her, a shroud sucking the life out of her spirit. In her later years, a slow neurodegenerative disease tortured and destroyed her. Through Ma, I learned time alone never heals but requires wisdom and compassion. Through Ma, I saw death could be merciful.

Sitting with Clara would always soothe my waves of sadness and quell the mutterings of my demons. They would be struck dumb by her majestic presence. I missed her when she moved to San Francisco. I had to follow her. Some would consider my actions strange, even a little demented. I did not care. I chose to follow my own reality. I could no longer stomach the mundane pursuits of career and material acquisitions. I needed time and space to reflect on a more meaningful life. I negotiated a sabbatical with my London-based employer and transferred to a position in their San Francisco office. I wanted a reprieve from my own pathetic suffering.

I learned I am a prisoner of my beliefs. Over ninety-five percent of my actions were driven by beliefs hiding deep in my subconscious, lurking as a secret army engaged in guerrilla warfare with my conscious self. I could always tell when one of their incendiary devices had been triggered because I would feel, for no other explicable reason, disempowered after a minor setback in life. The loss of self-confidence seemed real and lasting. At least Clara awakened me to the deceit.

I have learned that external circumstances, whether good or bad, make little difference to my inner peace. Only I can find freedom by transcending the lies of the ego, that part of me that says, 'You can't have what you want. Be grateful and settle for what you do have.' I had condemned myself to a life of mediocrity and heartbreak until Clara set me free. 'Never ever give up on your dreams,' she reminded me in

Golden Gate Park when I first arrived in San Francisco. I needed to sit near her, both of us, stone and flesh, bathed in sunshine. Those red roses were growing around her plinth again just like they had at Kew. Such vibrance, not the usual scarlet but a cool-toned, ruby shade against the white marble's translucence.

When does anger heal?

When it's a flash of awakening: old memories are cleansed of charged emotions and attendant beliefs exposed as false.

With Clara's help I could use anger for the greater good against the constant messages that women are nothing but whores to be possessed, used, and discarded by a deficient and degraded masculine. The mere thought that young women and girls are sexualised and brainwashed into being nothing more than an adolescent boy-man's plaything makes me seethe.

I did not know there are many other paths to feeling fulfilled in life besides the traditional path of career with marriage and children. If I could let go of harsh self-judgement, perhaps I could see other ways to live. Self-judgement and condemnation weaken my life force and damage any creative thinking. If only I could see that my life has been perfect even though I was unhappy at the time.

What if I did everything to the best of my knowledge and capacities at the time? What if my regrets are a waste of energy because I did not know then what I know now? Yes, of course, I may have made different decisions. I would not have started that relationship and saved myself a lot of pain. But, what if the awakenings since then could only have happened if I my heart was broken open? What if my foolishness was a gift I did not fully value? What if all has been, and remains, in perfect divine order?

Faith is like a rod of steel in the backbone, curving gently, providing support and strength to the most heartfelt inner knowing. The body's stance changes, becoming taller, softer yet resilient. The person is the same but a light from their soul shines through, rejuvenating their entire physical body. I often see the opposite in those who have lost faith in their dreams. Clara showed me. She awakened me. She is here to remind me who I am. I had forgotten long ago while living in a trance of toxic cultural messages: you are too old, too fat, too poor, too ethnic to be considered worthy. The danger is in believing these messages. It is a rare strength to value oneself independent of the judgements laden in these cultural norms. Being an outsider is a blessing for an artist. They remain uninfected by group attitudes and norms that would otherwise compromise their work.

I am not interested in seeking acceptance or validation by others. Clara has shown me the fallacy of that stance. She says the neediness for acceptance by others is shaky ground for any character. What if I do sound a little arrogant? Confident women are usually accused of arrogance by inadequate men. Clara has shown me a quiet self-confidence which, according to the Oxford English Dictionary, means *a feeling of trust in one's abilities, qualities, and judgement.* Self-confidence is not arrogance which means *an exaggerated sense of one's own importance or abilities.*

Clara speaks with Eleanor:
'Anything is possible with the divine. Remember, surrender.'
'What does it mean to surrender, Clara?'
'Hold on to your dreams and desires but let go of the belief that you know how they will manifest. Let go of any attempt to force a particular outcome. Let go of your ego as your guide in life. Instead of being

a wilful automaton in a meaningless pursuit of things, you become a channel for divine will.'

'I don't want to fail again, Clara. Stepping into the unknown scares me.'

'Be at peace. Listen to your heart. That is where you will know. Trust yourself.'

'How do I deal with fear and anxiety when I step into unknown territory?'

'There is no harm in acknowledging these feelings within you. You hinder your growth only when you grant these transient feelings supremacy over the higher, enduring wisdom of your heart. When the step to be taken is right, you may still feel fear and anxiety, but your heart will feel open, even excited. That is the sign to move forward despite the fear. If, however, your heart feels closed or even cold, even if you feel no fear, do not take that action. Stand firm in the faith that a better way will open up for you at the perfect time.'

'The fears are from my ego. I have been blinded by fear in the past and I have made decisions I now regret.'

'There is no need, Eleanor, for regret or sadness. Your blessing in life is to act from the truth of who you are. Whether you are an investment manager or leading an army into battle, acknowledge your fears but do not be directed by them. You still have choice in the matter. Our true character is revealed in times of uncertainty. All our pretences and illusions are burned away. A noble character will always prevail,' Clara said.

Her words soothed me.

'Eleanor, you are not a statue constrained by the rigidity of stone. Remember to breathe slowly and deeply into your body. It will ground you in your physical being and allow the frantic thoughts in your mind to fade away. The wisdom of your heart may be heard when the mind is still.'

'You were an enlightened ruler, Clara. Your people were lucky to have had you as their empress.'

'That was long ago. I ruled without wisdom. I made many mistakes as a ruler and as a woman.'

'You were only human, Clara. You must forgive yourself.'

'Yes, indeed I was. However, I was entrusted with a great responsibility – that of high office. My errors of judgement had fatal consequences for many innocent people.'

'Surely you have suffered enough?'

'My crimes weigh heavily on my soul. The angel Michael may grant me the power of forgiveness.'

'Whatever you have done, Clara, you are still worthy of love. Since I met you I have learned there is no such thing as coincidence. How can I become more conscious so I can do what's right?'

'Our failures as human beings are temporal. They are not spiritual failures. They are not forever. We are spared the full conscious awareness of them at the time because the gods deemed it cruel and unnecessary. We only learn of them when we have developed sufficient compassion and forgiveness to see them in their true light: these failures are but the milestones of an evolving soul.'

'All I can do is the best I can?'

'Being true to your higher self will help you avoid mistakes that may delay your growth. The course of your life may be likened to the construction of a large but intricate mosaic on a palatial wall. The overall theme and design is unknown except to the divine creator and is not revealed to you until the time is right. At significant times in your life, each tile is placed but not in order and not in the same location as previous tiles. It is impossible to make sense of the overall design at first when only a few tiles seem scattered across the bare wall. The gaps between the tiles are too big to see the overall picture. Over time, as you grow with new wisdom and experience, new tiles appear at strategic points in the overall design. The picture becomes clearer, the character chiselled, the destiny revealed.

A lack of foreknowledge is necessary because your life is a work of art. It is not a work of craft which relies on accepted ideas of substance and structure. Art requires the freedom to break rules, creating something not seen before. Knowing the design and form too soon, may cause you undue fear. Your ego may interfere. If the design is revealed before you are ready to bear the responsibility of that possible destiny, you may sabotage the work by ignoring subsequent guidance from your heart and suppressing leaps of your imagination. Your unique journey may be compromised and stymied. You may still have a good life, but it may lack a joyful quality leaving an inexplicable depression. The mosaic may still be a pretty design but may lack a divine sparkle and iridescence. A true work of art is breathtaking to behold regardless of the passing centuries or even millennia after its creation.'

'Is this why faith is so important?'

'Yes. Proceed with faith according to your heart's guidance. You are aware that you are not in a position to know everything in advance. Take that next step, trusting the necessary knowledge and insights will arrive at the perfect time.'

'Why does it feel like such a battle?'

'The battle is between the uncertainties in your mind and the growing surety of your heart. There will be peace when your heart is awakened and the tyranny of your rational mind is vanquished. The *Tao Te*

Ching states that mastering others is strength; mastering yourself is true power.'

'How on earth do I master myself? I feel broken, full of crap, conflicting beliefs, and impossible desires. Only when I am near you do I feel peace.'

'Sorrow seems to paralyse your spirit but, as with all emotion, it too shall pass. Be still and you may feel eternal joy masked beneath the sorrow that has broken open your heart. Remember, my dearest Eleanor, there exists a higher order to the chaos of your experience.'

'Will I ever see this higher order? There are days when everything seems dark, painful, and meaningless. I wander as though lost in a thundercloud.'

'On those days, spend time grounded in some physical but mind-free activity that reconnects you to the earth: go out for a walk near large trees or in a beautiful botanical garden; do any physical exercise that requires concentration but no thought; meet a good friend for coffee; have passionate sex with a man you trust, respect, and love.'

'Clara!'

'Of course, a wholesome masculine man is very grounding for an energetic woman such as yourself. It is time to relinquish your status as a celibate female.'

'No way. All my romantic misadventures have been a waste of my time and energy. My bitterness is beyond redemption. I have learned that my happiness is my responsibility. I used to look for happiness in other people, but I only set them up to disappoint me. An endless human drama. I am done with it.'

'Trust your awareness and transformation. This time you will not make the same mistakes as in the past.'

'How come?'

'You are stronger, wiser, and more aware of your needs and contribution in a relationship without being needy or afraid of being exploited.'

'I am sorry, Clara. The whole thing seems a minefield of unfulfilled expectations and heartbreak.'

'Not if you are clear who you are.'

'Who am I? I don't know anymore. My past mistakes cost me the chance of having children.'

'No, Eleanor, you were not destined to have children at that time.'

'With all due respect, Clara, I am a little over-the-hill now for motherhood.'

'Of course, in human-order thinking, you would be correct in your assessment. However, the divine works in ways beyond any human understanding.'

'You are talking about having faith?'

'Yes, the strength to hold on when circumstances suggest abandoning the dream.'

'Isn't that just blind faith?'

'No. You are watchful at all times for opportunities with a peaceful heart. There is no attachment.'

'What do you mean by attachment?'

'The mistaken belief you may be happy only if a particular outcome took place, if certain circumstances existed, or having a particular state of being in yourself or in others around you. The excessive need to be in control. The universe may have a more beautiful reality possible for you, but the fixation on the smaller goals and desires restricts the flow of grace – the magical quality where synchronicities take place with glorious abandon in your life. You demand another person shuts down their true self before you will accept them. This is not love but fear.

This is control. Conditions and demands on another person cause pain. Only love has the power to heal and transform.'

'Clara, why do I find this hard today? I feel restless. Weird emotions seem to engulf me. I am desperate for some peace.'

'Take physical exercise in nature. Fresh air and trees dissipate excess energies in your body as your consciousness transforms and awakens. Any physical activity that is wordless, rhythmic, and repetitive will soothe and still the mind, such as walking, running, swimming, horse-riding, skiing, or dancing.'

'It's as simple as that?'

'The human body is an energetic system controlled by thoughts both conscious and subconscious. Joyful forms of exercise that calm the mind, will clear and strengthen both mind and body.'

'I want to be useful. I want to serve without my pathetic human dramas getting in the way all the bloody time.'

'Allow what you desire for the world to also be a grace bestowed upon yourself.'

'It's OK to want prosperity and peace for myself?'

'You would be no use to the world without first-hand experience of these graces. It is a false choice to delay one's awakening because so many still suffer in the world.'

'But I would leave behind the very people I want to help.'

'Your transformation into your true self could inspire and release them to awaken sooner than if you held yourself back in some kindly, but misjudged, attempt to be of service. Not everyone will join you. Each person has their unique path, but your awakening could free them to follow their heart.'

'Why did it take me so long to see this?'

'You were not ready until now. You heard this wisdom in past lifetimes but were too attached to the dramas of your tribe to allow your own release and awakening.'

'Has my compassion been a weakness?

'Your compassion was misdirected. An innocent misunderstanding of the ways of spirit. Your compassion is a strength when tempered with clarity and wisdom. The world does not need more people who are full of sincere intentions yet who are not willing to embrace their own power and make changes in their lives. Any contribution is valuable, no matter how small, in alleviating the suffering of fellow beings. As your spirit evolves, you attract a more sublime heavenly guidance.'

'Does this happen with enlightenment?'

'One becomes light in being in terms of radiance and emotional weight, more receptive to divine guidance through intuition. One's body and spirit are no longer weighed down by dark, toxic beliefs or negative thought patterns. However, it is through confronting these dark beliefs and thought patterns that one's true divine nature is revealed.'

'Is this the dark night of the soul?'

'One is at last willing to face the dark beliefs that have imprisoned one's spirit, creating the same dramas over and over again.'

'What kind of dramas?'

'There are many based on false beliefs. Believing one is worthless, for example: lifetimes are spent in one form of enslavement or another whether to another person or government or an addiction to a substance. The possibilities are infinite.'

'Are you saying our beliefs create our realities?'

'We tend to think and act according to our beliefs and therefore we shape our personal circumstances. We only see what we believe. We ignore or discount anything we see that we do not believe.'

'Clara, that sounds outrageous. If we don't believe it, we won't see it? Hard to believe, though I'm sure it's true because of you. What about victims of circumstances?'

'A victim denies their own power and responsibility, creating the illusion of victimhood.'

'What about victims of natural disasters?'

'Usually, a cleansing and rebalancing of the earth's energies. People in tune with the planet may see signs warning of imminent disaster and move to safer areas. One cannot control all external circumstances. However, one can control one's reaction to them. Enlightenment is to be at peace, no matter what happens. What is troubling you today, Eleanor?'

'Life is slipping away from me. I feel far from ever achieving my goals.'

'Progress cannot always be measured in linear or logical ways. Continue working towards your goal in good faith even if the results do not seem to appear immediately. Be assured that your consistent thoughts and actions create a momentum in realms not perceived by the human mind but will nevertheless cause the manifestation of your desires at the perfect time.'

'Thank you, Clara. I do feel better. I'm a bit embarrassed I couldn't feel more serene today. Please excuse my anxious mind.'

'My dear Eleanor, the greatest illusion is the shame one experiences simply for being human.'

42

TRANSCENDENCE

~ Clara ~

For over a hundred years, I stayed in a country that has been defined by war. The Battle of Trafalgar fought in 1805 CE off the coast of Andalusia in Spain is now memorialised in London's Trafalgar Square. A battle fought in 1815 CE in modern-day Belgium now bestows its name on a busy London railway terminus: Waterloo Station. In both battles, Napoleonic forces were defeated.

Freedom is not free of charge. Freedom comes at a price. Some battles must be fought to ensure one's survival. The battles that disgust me are those fought for greed, for glory.

I fail to see the glory of battle that historians have pronounced throughout the ages. I see rivers of blood darkening the mud of the battlefield, or blackening the sea. In the stench of every word of glorious history, I hear only the screams of men and women dying far from home.

Political elites include the bankers and merchants of weaponry. They enrich themselves through the troughs of war. These purveyors of destruction do not know what they do. I feel no hatred for them now: they are a virus fed by my enemy, Xoran. I could do nothing in my ignorance. But that is my past. I no longer define myself by my failings. I was merely human.

What could I do now? A simple statue; a woman of stone? I am no longer a powerful ruler of a prosperous empire in alliance with equally prosperous, friendly neighbours. Today, I am nothing.

'You are everything, dear Clara,' said the angel now known as Michael. 'There is much you can accomplish. Still your mind and open your heart.'

My heavenly companion speaks wisdom beyond any human understanding. To argue with him would be futile. I am blessed by his presence despite my curse of stone. I would gladly remain stone for another twenty thousand years if only to have him by my side.

He reminds me, again, that is not my destiny.

In a world of grace, each government would be comprised of both a department or ministry of war as well as a ministry of peace. Departments of war are now named departments of defence. That word is more palatable to a governed people naïve in the ways of statecraft. Defending a country's security sounds more acceptable than warmongering to seize resources and increase the wealth of an unaccountable elite.

Xoran is a master at altering the language of things to diminish and even neutralise their emotion. The true impact of the language is denied. The most evil invention after the bomb is the euphemism. But perhaps it is the culture of euphemism that has given rise to the very invention of evil weaponry. Instead of stating, "civilians killed in a bombing raid", we now hear, "collateral damage sustained during a successful mission". Likewise, instead of "torture" we now hear the word "rendition". Humanity and responsibility are stripped out of the language and therefore out of our lives.

Wise rulers and generals avoid the hubris of war. They treat this foul language with disgust. They, too, smell the blood, the sweet stench of burning human flesh; they hear the screams; they see the unspeakable horrors of war.

A ministry or department of peace is charged with finding and inventing creative ways to resolve disputes, whether at home or overseas. They would work in partnership with military forces to ensure a country is rebuilt with resilient institutions that ensure peace. Peace cannot exist without clear systems of justice. A military force may be deployed to ensure order where there is no law until civil institutions are strong enough to assume their role.

My enemy is skilled: any kingdom he targets for his personal enrichment would find their governments undermined by corruption or even overturned. His spies and specialist mercenaries would know the target government's weaknesses and attack them. The people would be divided by laws designed to favour one group above another along the fault lines of colour, clan, creed, and sex. The peoples of the privileged ranks would blame those of the deprived ranks for the ills of their society without knowing that Xoran had rigged the government to draft policies that impoverish all to his and his allies' advantage. Poverty and war are no accidents of fate. Xoran found it easy to hide his strategies in plain sight. The people were too preoccupied with fighting and blaming each other to see the evil structured into their lives. Males would blame themselves for their economic failures in a system designed to enslave them. Their suicides would rise. Examining why would be deemed taboo in a society where males of a certain colour and creed ranked highest in an invented hierarchy.

Children of the deprived ranks would die with no explanation other than poverty. Anger would grow until civil unrest would manifest as violence in the streets. Xoran's allies would buy out the mining and resource exploration rights and property at low prices. He would choose his target kingdom with care: one rich in natural wealth, with an educated people, but with rulers who could be usurped if they failed to heed his counsel. Woe to those who underestimate his quiet manner. They find their kingdoms stolen from beneath their feet.

He has profited from living within the paradigm of fear. He has transcended fear himself and uses his wisdom as a weapon to prolong the suffering of those less fortunate. I have never learned the source of his greed. His desire to maintain rigid control perplexes me.

'He fears and hates the feminine,' said the angel called Michael. 'Those who embody the goddess – the unfolding of life in all its creative joy beyond the finite realms of the human mind. Remember, in his present incarnation as James, he witnessed his mother committing murder. A crime for which she was never brought to justice. He is driven to control everything. Every kingdom or realm that he ravages is both an act of anger at his father's weakness and vengeance for his father's death at his mother's hand.'

'How could I help him transcend his destructive consciousness?'

'That is not your task in this lifetime.'

'But, is compassion not the way?'

'His consciousness is unable to accommodate direct compassion in this lifetime.' Even in thought, the angel seemed serene. 'The way to defeat him is to engage him in battle once again.'

My stone form chilled, my translucence dimmed to ash grey as the London sky in November.

'Clara, be calm,' he smiled. 'Have faith. All is unfolding in perfect, divine order.'

So much love glowed through his eyes that my warmth and translucence soon returned. I have learned over the millennia, never to doubt his word. Those who can say this of their companions are fortunate beyond measure.

43

QUESTIONS

~ Clara ~

Eleanor came to visit me. I could not contain my joy at seeing her again. The afternoons were already shrinking in length as the summer rolled into fall. The seasons have their poetic moments too.

Eleanor brought a friend. My heart, though stone, came alive through the aeons of yearning at the sight of her companion, Richard.

'Beautiful, isn't she?' Eleanor said.

Richard was transfixed, his eyes wide in wonder.

'I *know* her,' Richard's voice was quiet.

My heart almost crumbled with pain at the sight of him. He seemed worn out by a life lived without passion, as though he had surrendered to an existence of meaningless struggle and penury. I could still recognise a glimmer of the same magnificent spirit behind the tired physical form. He was my Richard.

'Still your mind and open your heart and she will speak to you.' Eleanor's instruction brought more life to Richard's demeanour and bearing; his body straightened as though unwound. He became taller, his chest rose, and shoulders, once hunched, relaxed open.

'Clara? Where have I ...? Why?'

Poor Richard. He had too few words to serve the explosion of questions within him. I hesitated in my reply until his mind was still. I could feel his heart opening and expanding with a powerful love his current incarnation could not explain.

'Richard, with every ounce of my being, I love you.'

When the mind is cluttered and busy, it can only ask, 'Why?' When the mind is still, the soul's only reply is, 'Yes.'

Some days later Eleanor returned alone and recounted how they had met in a café near the City Lights bookstore. Richard was drawn to Eleanor in an effortless conversation and they quickly became friends. There was no romantic energy between them but there was a mutual recognition neither could explain. Eleanor thought intuitively to introduce Richard to me. In a world of grace, actions taken from the heart go beyond the realms of reason and logic.

He was an artist, a gifted sculptor and creator of masks for theatre and dance. He had abandoned his path. He was often plagued by bouts of depression that had no physical, psychological, or neurological cause.

Richard had accumulated much negative karma during his many lifetimes since the one he had shared with me. He had attracted and pursued many beautiful women who possessed a grace and an intelligence he found familiar. But he would soon abandon them. He caused untold suffering.

In this lifetime, Richard was unable to express his true passion – sculpture – believing such a profession would lead to his ruin. A closed heart meant circumstances, opportunities and resources shut down around him. Who would want to help and work with someone who resisted even the smallest first step?

Richard, in his current incarnation, was born into a wealthy, noble family and was living on a minimal trust fund. Minimal because he had cold relations with his family, one that could afford him opportunities he rebuked: he believed they were tainted with obligations and expectations he refused to fulfil. He thought his position principled and noble.

His family asked that he earn annually a sum equal to or in excess of his trust fund's annual payment. The logic was missing for him. He felt all money transactions reminded him of his family's hold over his life. He chose to struggle financially as well as spiritually.

Richard knew, in meeting me that day and standing before me, his fate was sealed. His awakening would come at a price, but he would make the required sacrifice.

What is the physiology of a broken heart?

Eleanor noticed how he had brightened and new life flowed through his body in meeting me in my stone form. He studied every sculpted fold of my robes and chiselled relief of my swords with the detailed eye only an artist may possess. Richard also recognised the signature work of a sculptor too similar to his own. The working with stone showed a brilliance and mastery beyond his attainment so far in this, his current, lifetime.

Little did he know, one of his many past lifetimes was as the impoverished English artist and sculptor, Marcus, living in Italy over a hundred years ago. In that cave near Monte Cassino, where my spirit had rested for nearly twenty-five thousand years, he sculpted my present form out of that boulder of pure white marble, unusual in that part of Italy. Richard today would have no conscious memory of that lifetime. Sudden irrational emotions may have given him clues. Deep in his unconscious mind, deep in his bones, hid memories of who he really was.

With every breath his mind asked, 'Why?'

With every breath his soul murmured, 'Yes.'

The question could only be resolved in his heart. His life became clear as his heart strengthened. Richard felt a new energy arising within him. The dormant power in his heart awakened on seeing me.

44

Darkness

~ Clara ~

No matter how deep my sadness and depression, I will find a way through the darkness to a new dimension. Every shadow within me I embrace with love and gratitude. Each one has been a gifted teacher.

I have met God in that darkness. God as the universal soul where my soul is one of an infinite variety. I have been disconnected for so long. I will emerge without taint of self-punishment or condemnation. The angel called Michael remains by my side. I am ready. He will guide me through my final battle. When the student is ready, the master appears. The same master has been with me all this time. He has now assumed a different aspect. That is all.

What have I done of any value in this world? What practical use have I been to humankind? At least I have done no more harm since my death on that day I refused to remember. Becoming stone cooled my overactive mind and extinguished the embers of anger. My heart now speaks in the stillness of eternity. The whisperings of my heart speak of Richard, my long-lost love. The whisperings speak of an elegant world of prosperity and peace. They speak of a dream much greater than I could ever accomplish alone.

'One person's dream could inspire millions of people and change the world for good,' Eleanor said. She had arrived by my side in silence while I was lost in thought. I should have realised Eleanor is an angel, too, but in human form.

'When many people have the same dream,' she added, 'no army in the world can stop them.'

'I wish I could raise an army to strengthen instead of destroy a dream.' Even though statues do not speak out loud, Eleanor could feel the heaviness of my words as they landed in her heart.

'All is not lost, Clara.'

'How so?'

The ground trembled in a familiar way beneath my plinth. I could feel the presence of the angel, Michael, nearby. He was silent and invisible to all around, but the trees shivered in delight. Despite Eleanor's spiritual training, an angel appearing out of the ground and towering over her could overwhelm her heart's electromagnetic field and cause a cardiac arrest. Michael was being discreet as usual.

'Feels like there's a big angel hanging around,' Eleanor said.

I could feel Michael smile.

'You are indeed perceptive today, Eleanor.' It was good to see her again. But how does one introduce an earthly friend to an angel? What is the correct protocol?

Is there such a protocol?

Of course there is no need for protocol in matters of direct communication with the divine. When the heart is ready, meetings with divine entities are effortless. The mystical traditions are clear on this since the beginning of humankind. Wisdom texts from ancient times speak of this universal experience.

'Aren't you going to introduce me, Clara?' Eleanor said.

Michael duly appeared in all his glory. He submerged his towering height into the ground up to his neck so we could see into his eyes. The air was electrified. Eleanor felt a firm pressure in her chest and heard a whining ring in both ears. She felt a popping in her ears as the atmospheric pressure changed. She approached and kissed Michael on his cheek.

Michael was not accustomed to being kissed by a human being, but he appreciated the gesture.

45

RADIANCE

~ Clara ~

Where will this story take me? I am the narrator. I am supposed to be omniscient and magisterial. Some days, I feel stuck in this stone form despite its translucent beauty. Within this rigid, crystalline structure my dreams are stored too securely. They may be released by enchanting me with sacred words of the correct frequency.

At dusk, with faint stars emerging, I feel the power of the poet's words: stand firm with a soft and open heart.

'Time to dance and sing,' Michael said. He loved to tease me. He was not made of stone. He was made of nothing but energy; he could be nothing and everything. I envied and feared his formlessness in equal measure. 'Time for you to live again in human form,' he said. 'You will live many lives in one to compensate for the millennia in stone. You will experience many wonderful emotions.'

'I will live again?'

'The woman you were in your past cannot guide you in your future. She died in despair on that battlefield long, long ago.'

'Then who am I?'

'You invent yourself anew. Acknowledge your sorrows and regrets but do not dwell on them. Allow them to fade away. You are ready.'

I was bewildered by his words, but soon enough I felt liberated by them. He is a powerful angel after all. I soon realised not every statue is blessed with such a presence.

'You are ready to face him.' Michael's words were gentle enough, though I found his message hard to bear. 'Trust who you are now: a woman of great wisdom and courage. You only fear what you do not know about yourself.'

What a fool I was to even try to argue with an angel, especially one like Michael. I reasoned and argued with him for five thousand years before I realised there was neither right nor wrong. In his patient smile I glimpsed another, much higher, consciousness eluding me until I surrendered my limited reason and allowed his words into my heart. Now, I understand: in the beginning was the word.

A new world began when the angel's words first resonated in my heart. My subsequent actions would be inspired by that new world within me.

'Make time, not excuses, for the important things in life. Breathe and slow down,' said Michael. 'Find inspiration in the struggle and your dreams will soar as our eagle friends, Aurora and Polaris, on a warm, sunny afternoon.'

My imperial battalion, my warriors, are searching for me. They know I cannot fight this battle alone. Thousands of statues of ancient warriors have been discovered in central Asia. A few of these statues have been shipped to England and are in a sold-out exhibition at the

British Museum in London. My warriors are a thousand of the finest statues discovered and too precious to risk damage in transit to the USA. Historians assumed they were young male warriors. Taller than the average stone warrior found and of lithe build, the historians failed to notice the feminine curves in their breastplates.

The statues were instead replicated in a fine-textured rose-grey granite quarried in the state of New Hampshire. The detailed specifications were sent from Tehran in present-day Iran, once part of ancient Persia, in a brave collaboration with an American museum and advanced technology venture.

The thousand replicated statues are on their way to San Francisco and will marshal in Golden Gate Park in the guise of a great public outdoor exhibition of Asian art and history:

The Graceful Dead – The Stone Warriors of Ancient Persia.

Only where there is death, can there be life. The art installation would inspire peace and understanding across many peoples and nations. The statues were all sold in advance to art collectors around the world who would take delivery after the exhibition ended in late fall. Vibrant secondary and even tertiary markets for the statues arose out of those who did not secure an initial order but sought to buy out the art collectors, even before delivery, at many times the original price.

Each statue of my imperial guard had a unique sigil – a symbol sculpted in stone that possessed powers to invoke the spirit of the ancient warrior. The thousand sigils were deemed sacred and were not to be shared with the Americans for a mere art installation. The art authorities in Tehran intended to send the statues' data to San Francisco, omitting the unique sigil on each statue's breastplate and replacing each one with a generic symbol instead. However, the appropriate electronic file was named incorrectly and the American art museum received the complete sigil data. By the time the Tehran authorities had discovered the error, the statues were already replicated and marshalled in Golden Gate Park. Each replicated statue had on its breastplate a unique sigil reproduced in exquisite detail.

I did not call them. My fervent wish would be never to endanger them again.

'Clara, it is their desire to serve you.' Michael was still by my side.

'I thought the woman they once served died long ago?' I could not bear more destruction in my name.

'Yes, she is dead, but they wish to serve you today. You will hear them calling you to lead them once more.'

My heart seemed to swell. Waves of unknown emotions bubbled in my chest: some would say love, humility, belonging, and, gratitude for being forgiven by so many souls. It has been an eternity. I have missed each and every one of them.

One question gnawed at my heart.

'Why did they become statues? Were their souls not released to heaven on their deaths?'

'They chose to follow you in your fate. Their souls would not rest.'

A warm knot of pain opened in my heart. My stone form trembled.

'Rest now, Clara. Xoran will visit soon.'

46

ENTERTAIN THE THOUGHT

~ Clara ~

My swords, Clarity and Brilliance, were unlike any other exquisite possession. They brought power and regeneration to their rightful bearer. To the wrongful they brought certain disaster. They have been missing for thousands of years. Who stole them away from Xoran the night after the day I refused to remember?

It takes a mighty angel to defeat a demon. An angel may act only with the permission of the human under their guidance and protection. I am willing to face Xoran again even though I am frightened. I do not know when or how we will meet. The Angel of Compassionate Condemnation, now known as Michael, reassures me that answering my questions now would not enlighten me. It is too soon. My consciousness will rise to meet the challenge. I will be ready.

The Angel Michael has stood by me for thousands of years. He will not leave me but asks that I stand firm for my true self by following my heart's guidance. I will regain my strength and sense of purpose. The guilt and shame fade as shadows sliding off my soul.

Entertain the thought that I am ignorant of what is truly possible. What if the only obstacles on my path are the beliefs I hold about everything? What a gift life is truly: a journey of exploration and magic, becoming a conduit of divine energy.

Michael reminds me to practise mindfulness at all times. Practice trains the mind to synchronise with the heart, creates coherent energy in the body, and provides power for any intention. In this way, a simple wish from the heart manifests without suffering. The effort is in the discipline of a mind trained to be still and obey the heart. Extraneous limiting beliefs are transcended. New beliefs are integrated into one's being. This is sacred work. I am grateful, privileged, and honoured to be here.

Entertain the thought I am guided at all times: all my needs are met if I follow my heart for the highest good of all.

The opiate of the people was once religion but now it is the cult of celebrity and notoriety: that desperation for fame and external validation without any desire to serve others through a creative contribution of one's own. The cult of celebrity is a useful distraction for any government seeking to control the minds of the people. Another distraction is blaming the poor and immigrants for all social ills – a sign of a government defrauding its people. It would be catastrophic for any corrupt government if people united to fight injustice, regenerate our planet, and avert the never-ending global wars.

This world is more than I could ever comprehend. Everything has a rational explanation though our present civilisation may not yet have the required scientific knowledge for such an explanation. It may not yet have the wisdom. The unexplained is brushed aside, unworthy of further investigation for fear of powerful commercial interests and damage to the scientist's reputation.

Entertain the thought that all pain and suffering can be healed. The events from the past that once haunted me can be embraced with compassion and acceptance.

47

SEPTEMBER

~ Michael ~

The swords, Clarity and Brilliance, disappeared around 23,000 BCE. A world where these swords would have stood guard would have been one of prosperity, peace, and phenomenal beauty. Doubt and confusion would be but passing clouds unable to find themselves at home.

Doubt and confusion are a natural consequence on a path of growth and learning. Under the guidance of an enlightened master, they may signal a whole new life rich in understanding and compassion as old thoughtforms fade away. But when doubt and confusion are constant conditions designed to render an intelligent people compliant as frightened sheep, people can neither trust themselves nor trust each other. And they cannot discern true ideas and events from falsehood.

The swords choose their human custodian with care. As sacred pieces of an unknown ancient history, the diamonds alone are priceless. How do archaeologists investigate the history of relics with no clue to their origin? Their discovery would create more questions. The diamonds were faceted in the most advanced cut then, more brilliant than any known today.

The sword Clarity is set with a walnut-sized violet diamond in its pommel while Brilliance is set with a blue-white diamond. Each flawless diamond is set into its respective pommel with simplicity and elegance. The fire within each flawless diamond is spectacular even in low light. The swords represent wisdom and compassion.

They were discovered two months earlier in an ancient temple vault unearthed in the city of Isfahan in northern Iran. At the June Solstice, a shaft of sunlight at the perfect angle revealed the swords' sarcophagus. Clara's swords were looted by a unit of mercenaries intending to trade them for a consignment of heroin from Afghanistan. The country had fallen into disarray – another casualty of Mr James A. W. Shield III with his direct contacts in the region disguised as defence contractors and military advisers. As a collector of military relics he agreed to buy them at the bargain price with little negotiation. He would feign ignorance and surprise at the irregularity of payment but would accommodate his counterparty through his collaborators in the Afghan opiate trade. James understands the temporal power of ancient artefacts: memories of the former bearer held in the metal exude an inestimable influence in the here and now.

The swords' true beauty and splendour remain hidden, even the scabbards appearing as dull alloy yet still exquisite in form. The steel, diamonds, and rubies sleep behind their dark grey mask, protected, spellbound. The mercenaries tried to drive up the price by affirming the swords' rare value and how they once belonged to an ancient warrior who ruled a lost empire. They even went as far as to state that The legendary Swords of Aurelia would shine with a brilliance as bright as the sun when brought near a true likeness of their former bearer, bestowing untold power and wealth when some comet returns.

When he received word from his broker, James laughed at the attempt to cajole more money from him but admired the mercenaries' imaginative ploy. As a gesture of goodwill, he raised his bid by five percent as the items on offer seemed authentic decoys forged in the same era as the legendary swords instead of the usual thousand-year-old reproductions.

Little did he know the legend also spoke of a strange curse.

And so it was, Clara's swords made their way from the remains of an ancient empire in deepest Asia to the capital city of a modern mighty nation, Washington, D.C. The swords would become James's possessions just as they had once been in his prior incarnation as King Xoran. They reached US soil in one of the many discreet official pouches on board a US Air Force jet landing at a military base in Maryland.

48

PEACE II

~ Clara ~

There is order at every level of existence.

There is harmony on the inter-galactic scale as well as the nano-scale of the chemistry and quantum physics of life. For peace to exist on Earth, it is our responsibility to live in accordance with the harmony inherent in all matter and energy.

In the late twentieth century there were three revolutions: quantum mechanics (the motion and interaction of sub-atomic particles); information or computer technology; and biotechnology.

In the 1980s, scientists thought it impossible to sequence the human genome before 2015, but with the revolution in computing hardware and software, where prices fell while computing capacity rose, the work was completed in the year 2000.

What could be possible with clean, low-cost energy within the next generation?

49

THE WISE RULER RETURNS

~ Clara ~

The swords will find their way to me through James's avarice. I can no longer hide. They have slipped away never to return. I was once a ruler of a great people. It is in their memory that I act today.

'It is in your memory that they are here today,' said the angel beside me. Michael has decided he is no longer the angel of compassionate condemnation. That, he says, was his disguise. He assumes another role as my self-appointed guide, but I am not clear what he intends. That is the mystery of Michael. My purpose, he insists, is to allow and accept the many imminent blessings.

A statue's rigidity is a weakness not a strength. The wisdom to stand firm with a soft and open heart is the foundation beneath a palace of many blessings. With Michael beside me what further blessings could I possible desire?

'Gratitude flows from an abundant heart.' His smile intrigued me as usual. I could do nothing but wonder at the realms beyond my understanding. What worlds of wisdom could he see where I am still blind? I remember the ancient saying: when the student is ready, the master appears. The student is ready when her current consciousness can no longer assuage the many questions arising from her soul. The student is ready when her thirst for wisdom can no longer be quenched with her bone-tired knowledge and ideas. The master appears when the student is willing to wait in the world of the unknown no matter how fearful that world may seem.

Human beings fear what they do not understand, but the wise embrace the mystery instead of refuting it. The heart can embrace more than the conscious mind can fathom. Usually, the heart listens and accepts immediately, while the mind needs time to expand in consciousness to accommodate the new world of being. Faith allows the expansion of consciousness. A fearful, overactive mind would shut down growth. When no logical or rational thoughts can help, the wise keep an open mind, receptive to ideas that come out of the deep superconscious – a state connected to intuition and divine wisdom.

Allow time for the deep-seated changes to take place in my mind and body. This is faith – the stillness without need of certainty. A powerful desire from my heart fuels this faith, a desire from the soul seeking joyful expression in the world of matter. Without this desire, my faith would crumble to suit the vagaries of circumstance.

My faith was weak. Until I saw my enemy's plans for the new world, my faith was almost non-existent. I can see the terrible consequences of his proposed actions: humans rendered docile and compliant by advanced technology and thwarted medicine; sentient beings hybridised with machines, their spirits neutered, controlled, and cut off from their divine birthright.

My enemy has awakened me.

50

A COMET

~ Clara ~

'The comet of Aurelius will return within days. It will shine bright and strike terror in this world. Do not be afraid. The comet that once foretold your doom, on that battlefield long ago, now heralds your destiny,' Michael said.

Michael's words did not bring me joy. The hour of my liberation was at hand yet I was scared beyond death. My faith in Michael's teaching and guidance gave me strength to stand firm in my otherwise shaken serenity. My warriors were with me, marshalled only a few hundred metres away in the park. Eleanor agreed to conduct the prayer ceremony. Michael and I will guide her when to start the ceremony to coincide with the comet's arrival. At the perfect time, Eleanor will feel an urge to take action. She will feel a quiet insistence from heart. Her body will feel expansive and peaceful – a trait of genuine divine guidance in those whose hearts are open. False guidance is laced with cold fear, anxiety, and even compulsion: actions are driven by a hyperactive mind, constricting the human body and causing disease.

A poet knows the power of sacred words. She will choose and recite the most powerful of them. She will release me from my private hell.

'Clara, you will know how to proceed. Breathe as you disembody. Your human aspect may feel fear and apprehension because your spirit has lived for an aeon in the illusory safety of stone.'

'Even though I am afraid, I have faith and will heed your guidance,' I said, but my fears had another dimension. 'Will I lose you by my side once I am no longer stone?'

'You are an infinite being,' Michael said. 'Living within the confines of your marble form was a limitation you had chosen at the end of your last human lifetime. I will never leave you unless you request otherwise.'

'Never, ever leave me. Please.'

51

INTERSTELLAR

~ Clara ~

We are star matter. We are star energy. My civilisation once harnessed the power of our closest star, the sun. This is not a fiction of science but an ancient science lost long ago. My people understood the laws of energy, of matter, and the nature of life.

How does such a civilisation disappear from all knowledge or record? Meteors, asteroids, or comets collide with our planet destroying entire cities as though nuclear weapons were detonated. Wars may devastate civilisations. Every piece of heritage, every page of knowledge – treasuries of learning may be lost forever. It has taken humans nearly twenty thousand years to even contemplate the existence of civilisations more advanced than those present. It is assumed that these advanced civilisations are on other earth-like planets in similar solar systems millions of light-years away from our own. One light-year is 5.879 trillion miles or exactly 9,460,730,472,580,800 metres.

How could our civilisation be alone in the vastness of our galaxy?

I am still unable to comprehend what happened to my people. The millennia swept by. Time seemed a whirlwind, destroying everything in its wake. Countries disappeared beneath newly formed deserts. Peninsulas broke away and sank into the sea after earthquakes beneath the ocean floor.

Coastlines changed with every millennium. Frontiers were drawn and redrawn many times, swallowing smaller realms in the way. The ones that survived to this day are nestled high in mountain ranges. They are accessible only by narrow trekking roads unfit for any mechanised infantry division and deemed to be of no strategic interest.

Civilisations that flourished knew how to transcend the dangers of weather and natural disasters. They could control the weather for the benefit of all. Today, we are changing our weather by, for example, damaging our rainforests. Their transpired water vapour settles on the ocean, cooling the surface in the summer, and minimising the risk of hurricanes.

Weather-related disasters are a sign of disharmony as the earth seeks to regain balance. The very word disaster means against the stars.

Harmony is the law of love according to European philosopher and alchemist, The Count of Saint Germain. Love cannot breathe through beings wired for fear. Life force in the body cannot flow. Fearful resistance needs tremendous energy and usually forces the being into decline. Realignment reinvigorates and rejuvenates because harmony is true. Love is true. Fear is a reaction to a lie.

Wars have not all been destructive. Some wars enriched cultures through an appreciation of different ways of life. Some wars forced entrenched and secluded cultures to breathe, sharing their gifts with the rest of the world. Some wars forced the swift decline of over-reaching empires that had lost their way in dissolute bureaucracy.

Empires that prospered were those that stood for inspiring ideals and values that were far beyond the personal interests of a parasitic elite class. Thriving empires stand for the flourishing and transformation of all sentient beings.

Today, our planet hungers for leaders who think beyond short-term national interests. They see socio-economic systems working in harmony for the benefit of all. They do not speak to avoid blame nor in turn to blame their predecessors. These leaders speak from a profound commitment to a greater vision. They seek to embrace the legacies of their predecessors and bequeath, with care, fine legacies to their successors. They know yesterday's solutions create today's problems, and therefore, assigning blame is ridiculous.

It is time to reconsider how we use our planetary wealth. Two thirds of known oil reserves are in the Persian Gulf – a notoriously unstable region of the world, and kept deliberately so by none other than my enemy. He knows that a country rich in desirable resources and weakened political systems is easier to exploit, easier to invade and occupy. He mitigates the risks using taxpayer's money to finance the required military operations. He reaps the rewards through private concerns which he and his allies control.

What will it take to remove the power of the merchants of fossil fuels, the purveyors of enslaved medicine and science, their financiers, and their political friends? Once the suppressed clean energy and healing technologies are released, our planet will be transformed within a generation.

We will leave behind the fossil-fuel age as we left behind the ages of stone, iron, and bronze. We will enter an age of abundant, low cost, clean energy.

We will enter the interstellar age.

52

SPEAK TO ME

~ Memoir ~ Author ~

Speak to me, woman of stone.

Where have you gone? Why can't I hear you?

I miss our conversations. I miss hearing your lovely voice in my heart. I miss feeling the angel's smile near me. Have I stepped into some other dimension and lost you?

No, you say, all is going to plan. Just wait and see.

OK, but I am scared I'll screw up.

No, I won't, you say, because this is the writing faith: the ability to continue writing through the doubt and confusion inevitable on this path. And that, you say, is my strength and power – the courage to continue.

What more is there to say on my part? I can only sit here in silent gratitude.

An hour or so passes. The author sits in peace then leaves to have lunch and go to her day job.

Author returns to the page at 23:15 GMT that evening.

There is an ebb and flow to writing. Some days, no matter what, no words will come. All the characters have gone to a meeting at an unknown location. The author has no idea they have gone. She's losing her mind. She speaks openly about the disappearance of the characters to her sympathetic colleagues and friends.

Next day (12:35 GMT, Wednesday 28 November 2007), author faces the page again for an hour before going to her day job.

Serenity is a gift bestowed on the courageous. Today is the tenth anniversary of my divorce from my first and only husband, Gary. My subsequent romantic relationships have been painful. I always second-guessed myself and never had the courage to follow my heart's desire.

Today, I awoke from a deep sleep with the resolve to take care of myself and the realisation that I would rather be single for the rest of my life than compromise my dreams of being with the one. I write about a deep, enduring romantic love between a man and a woman that transcends all human ideas of time yet I cannot believe such a love could exist for me in my present lifetime.

Therein lies the conflict in writing this book. In the past ten years I have had romantic encounters with a few men. Each one has brought me the gift of personal growth. Two years ago, the last gentleman in particular brought me great healing at a time of spiritual crisis. Since then, I have been celibate, not through any arduous discipline but from a desire to remain untouched. I had become a woman of stone, grieving for the children I never had. Today my grief has abated. I have since learned from many parents that children can be as much a source of sorrow as of joy. I have learned that the only way to allow true love into my heart is to be true to myself first as in the immortal words of William Shakespeare:

*"This above all: to thine own self be true,
And it must follow, as the night the day,
Thou canst not then be false to any man."*

Author goes to her day job then to her friend's house for supper that evening and gets a little drunk on champagne.

The next day, Thursday, 29 November 2007:

I have been an abject failure in love and romance. The fire within me has never really shone so how could my true love ever find me? Moulding myself to fit the expectations of others never worked. The safety was illusory.

My cowardice has been more dangerous than finding the courage to be my true self in the first place.

Forget the self-pity and the fear,
Follow my desire,
and finish writing this book.

53

TENSION

~ Memoir ~ Author ~

Tension is part of being alive. Tension is needed to wield a sword when fighting doubt and confusion. Not all tension is useful.

I am so bored with this. There must be some other opening to this bloody chapter. What is missing now? What do I need to get this book complete? All I hear are the odd words like "tension" as though part of a riddle. I am not a cryptographer. I need to hear stories I can understand and write down. I cannot sit for hours producing just a few sparse lines. There must be another way. I pray to the angels to help me help Clara get her story down. All the characters seem to have gone. Where is Clara? Where are David, James, Richard? What is Eleanor up to now?

'My story is your story too.'

'Oh my God, Clara. There you are at last. Look, I have no idea what I am doing. I just show up at the page as promised but I am dry. I have no ideas. There's no flow at all.'

'There is a rhythm to writing as in all things. This week has been good training in your resilience, endurance, and discipline. Do not fail me now.'

'I will not fail you. I will complete the promised number of hours this week.'

'Next week we will write in a different way that encourages creativity and flow. This week it was necessary to sit and write when there seemed nothing for you to write about. Your consciousness needed this time to grow and your heart to strengthen and expand.'

'I see the story is going to heat up pretty soon, especially now that your swords have arrived on US soil. I will need to be ready.'

Clara smiles at me with compassion.

'I am ready,' I corrected.

54

THE PROMISE

~ Memoir ~ Author ~

All the characters have been silent during this week's writing sessions. Are they waiting for me, the author, to wake up in some way?

Am I doing something wrong?

Have I missed something?

'No, Angela. All is well,' Clara said into my heart. 'You are in a powerful transition at this time. Receiving more story material may be too much for you to bear.'

'Of course, I have recently started an intense meditation course. I didn't realise that would bring the writing to a standstill.'

'Writer's block is nothing to fear. However, we do not wish for you to go insane through writer's overload where a writer attempts to assimilate more information than their psyche or creative capacity can bear. But that will not happen as we are watching you carefully.'

'Thank you, Clara. Writing can be lonely. I'm scared I don't know how this book will ever get done.'

'You do not need to know how. Speak to me in your writing, Angela. No matter how you feel, I will listen. I will never judge you. My story is your story too.'

55

WRITING DOWN THE STORY

~ Memoir ~ Author ~

'Clara, where are you? I am struggling here. Come on, help me out a little.'

'You are doing well enough alone. You do not need me.'

I could feel the warmth of her enigmatic smile. I swear she was getting worse than the angel. Clara was playing with my limited understanding and consciousness. Her playfulness, however, was always devoid of malice.

'Spend your time and energy wisely. Minimise distractions. Read only for inspiration.'

'But Clara, I feel so dry. No ideas whatsoever. Hard to sit and write when I feel so cut off from the flow.'

'This is the writing faith. Come to the empty page on your laptop and type out your heart's yearnings and dreams. Allow them to pour out of you. Do not worry about anything making sense. You will have a completely new understanding of the writings when you come to edit them in the future.'

'I just wish it would flow out of me and be done with it. I know I am impatient. I see the odd tantalising lead in the story, then nothing. I have never written a book before. I don't really know what to expect.'

'Being in the unknown is hard at times. This is the writing faith. Show up each day at the page and write your heart out. Expect changes in your life very soon that will allow the flow to become easier. In the meantime, breathe and write one word at a time, one phrase at a time. That is all.'

On Tuesday morning, 4 December 2007, the author visits a trusted spiritual clairvoyant and clairaudient in north London who is experienced in helping authors through writer's block.

I had met Adrienne on two other occasions in the previous twelve months. She came highly recommended by my friend, Helen, a fellow writer. On a grey Tuesday morning, in early December 2007, I took two buses from south-west London where I lived to Adrienne's home in north London – a two-hour journey.

The Tube, also known as The London Underground, would have been faster. I just could not tolerate that stench. An oily odour still lingered in the warm stagnant air of the Tube trains and tunnels after the suicide bombings two years earlier that killed fifty-two people and injured more than seven hundred and seventy.

In Adrienne's bright and airy sitting room, I selected a dozen or so cards from her seventy-eight-card tarot deck. I spread the deck out into a fan shape, cards face down on the compact desk between us. The emerald-green tablecloth felt soft beneath my fingertips. With Adrienne's permission, I switched on a small digital voice-recording device.

Smartphones were not yet widely available. The first ever iPhone had only been released that summer.

'Choose with your left hand. That's the psychic one,' she said. Her chirpy Scottish accent and cheerful manner always put me at ease. 'Writers are psychic and channel information from the spirit world. My guides are telling me you are channelling information you may not understand yet. Don't worry. It will all make sense later. Open up, relax and let it flow.'

Adrienne turned over one of the cards I had chosen. 'Fear of success is blocking your writing. Hidden fears of not deserving success. Doors will fly open when your book is published and you will give up some privacy and control of your life. Do not be frightened. You'll get the level of success you can cope with.'

That was reassuring. One of the reasons I booked this session with Adrienne was to find out if there were any hidden blocks to my writing and progress in life in general.

'Yoga, meditation, and breathing exercises will help,' she added. 'Be flexible with meditation: demons will come up for healing and release. We all have them from childhood, our ancestral lines, previous lives. Something like reiki, reflexology, and aromatherapy will help to clear blocked spiritual channels connecting your mind, body, and spirit.'

Adrienne turned over another of the cards I had chosen. 'Five of wands: danger of your energy levels dropping over winter. Tune in and listen to your body and rest when you need to. You're becoming more intuitive with your body and your health. Don't force your way through fatigue as your body may be fighting viruses. Get rest when you need to.'

'Pink satin ballet shoes? Why are they showing me this?' Adrienne said. Her spiritual guides could be as perplexing as Clara is with me. 'I see a ballerina on her toes. Something about endurance and strength. They're telling me dance is extremely important for you. I see you doing something like salsa or ceroc – a fast high-energy dance.'

Adrienne did not know I had been taking lessons in Argentine Tango. My favourite dance. In London I felt too socially awkward to dance with strangers who were unforgiving of my novice missteps. In San Francisco, the dance scene was more friendly, more fun. I could relax and dance. Argentine Tango is a moving meditation. Sometimes, when I moved intuitively with a fine dance partner, the experience was magical.

'Don't worry about being blocked in your writing. It's temporary. Your consciousness is clearing out a lot of old energies. It's only a pause.

'Love is being called out. A serious relationship is there for you but the book comes first. Get the book finished. He will have children already. You will join a lovely family. It will not be an easy route to publishing the book. The serious relationship and publishing the book will happen all at once.

'Nine of wands: the card of travel. Really important for you as it will give you an almost enlightened creativity.

'Ten of pentacles: it's a wish card. There are only two in the whole deck. This one is about career and material success. Excellent cards drawn. It always amazes me that people draw the perfect cards that reflect their lives.

'Two of cups: you need love in your life, but there is still someone you have not gotten over, though you are much better. You will move on by this time next year. He still thinks about you – a strong karmic link between you. He's a Gemini. They're are a bit dangerous because they're mentally powerful. They can switch off their emotions and be cold, manipulative, and almost amused by the distress they cause in others. He hasn't let go of you either. Hate to say this, but you will meet him in another life.'

'Oh God almighty, not again. How many more lessons do I have to learn?' I almost groaned. Our relationship had ended four years earlier.

'I know, but he has to learn lessons as well. This is the thing, you've known him in previous lives. We do keep meeting up with the same people life after life, but it will be another chapter, like your book, where you both will have grown, changed, and learned lessons. I bet he owes you karmically, emotionally.

'Four of wands: you'll get over Mr Gemini. You're in the last lap. Sometimes the last lap is the hardest. You'll be completely clear of him next year.

'I keep being drawn to the King of Pentacles,' Adrienne said.

'That's Helen's favourite card too,' I said. 'I can tell her we both got him in our readings.' Adrienne and I let out a hearty chuckle.

'They're usually earth sign energies,' she said. 'Strong Capricorn energy. Aries, too, in his chart. He is dynamic. Money is important to him. Very practical. Ambitious. Connected with writing. Maybe he's a writer too. We don't get told everything for our own good.

'Five of swords: about discipline. You are very good about setting aside time to write. This card is about your parents. Certain dynamics in the family will shift. Eventually, you will become the parent, particularly to your mother. You will swap roles.'

'That's happening now. I've already started nagging Ma. Whenever she lights a cigarette in the kitchen I ask her if she really needs yet "another cigarette". Then we both laugh.'

'Her lungs have taken a hammering,' Adrienne said. Her tone darkened. 'I feel she really does need to stop, even if she can bring it down to five cigarettes a day. I don't want to scare you, but she has damaged her health quite significantly. I am drawn to emphysema.'

'Will definitely tell her that when I get home,' I said. Ma could be so stubborn. I wasn't sure relaying this message to her would make much difference.

'The Tower Card: a huge upset is coming. There will be a price to pay for her smoking. Your mother will be forced to change once her health takes a turn for the worse.

'The World Card is a very positive card. A karmic cycle is ending. You're still in the process of transformation. I see a caterpillar turning into a butterfly. This is on many levels. On one level it's about your book, but every level of your life is changing like your relationships and your writing.

'Even though The Tower and the Five of Swords are very difficult cards, they are about huge growth experiences and you will benefit long-term.'

Adrienne drank more water from the two-litre bottle on the table. Spiritual work was dehydrating. The session was complete.

I rose from the chair to get my coat. The digital voice recorder had stopped working despite the full battery indicator. Something had disabled its electronic brain.

'Clara! She's here,' Adrienne shouted, her eyes opened wide, mouth open in a huge smile. Adrienne's chest lifted as she turned and looked towards a presence by the window. I could neither see nor hear anything, but to Adrienne, the presence was as clear as day.

'Clara is so happy to communicate with you out in the open at last. A thousand years ago, in a past life, you were both priestesses in a Temple of Isis. Clara was your senior and teacher. You were devoted to her.' Adrienne could barely breathe out the words. Her body shook with joy. 'Clara doesn't need to incarnate anymore. She's now an ascended master, a goddess even. She's laughing at the very idea.'

I left Adrienne's home. It was early afternoon. I boarded a bus south towards London Bridge and then another bus home to Streatham. The two-hour journey was the same as before, in reverse. But this time, from my seat on the upper deck of the 43 bus, nothing seemed real. Bankers, brokers, lawyers, journalists were going about their business in The City, London's financial district. In the usual sea of grey and navy-blue suits, a blonde woman in a red coat stomped her way through lunch-time lolling office workers. Her face was hard, shoulders set, her eyes narrowed in anger. I recognised her. It was Jane. She was an editor at a large financial news agency nearby. We had met on a writing course in Italy a few years earlier and became friends. She had since lost interest in our friendship. Can't say I blamed her. My insecurities and confusion would have put off any one as confident and ambitious as she was. I hated to imagine what had made her so angry that day.

The people, the suits, and the places I saw from the bus now existed in another dimension; one where I would no longer return.

That evening, Clara speaks to the author:

'Angela, now I know you finally understand. Today has been a turning point in your life. You are forever transformed. You have learned that I, Clara, am a real spiritual being, not an invention of your imagination. There is no longer any reason to doubt yourself nor the words you hear through your heart. The energy and the ideas come through you from me but you bring them to life.

'We live by stories. Dry facts and figures inspire no one. All the data in the world cannot inspire the fulfilment of a long-held dream. A dream is independent of external conditions. The most powerful dreams are those that come from within and can withstand the onslaught of negative beliefs from both within and without. The most dangerous enemy is always self-doubt.'

'I will never doubt you again, Clara.'

'You never doubted me. You only doubted yourself. That has ended. I am happy and relieved.'

'I am a very lucky woman.' I said, 'I feel like the richest woman on earth.'

'*That,*' Clara said, 'is spiritual wealth.'

56

CLARA IS REAL

~ Memoir ~ Author ~

Clara is real. I know now. She is a real spiritual being. Clara is not a mere invention of my rampant imagination: she is a goddess of great beauty and light. She is far too modest to describe herself this way but I feel those energies around me when she is near.

I long to hear her voice clearly, not as a psychosis but as a gift of regular spiritual practices like meditation. I love typing what I feel she is saying. Touch typing, for me, is easier than writing by hand. Clara first came to me at a distressing time in my life, but I feel she has been by my side always. Clara only made herself known when she felt I was ready to hear her voice and feel her presence.

At that distressing time, when all I had held dear in my life I chose to let go, Clara's voice in my heart would comfort me. I would not be alarmed: all my structures of belief were falling away. Who was I to say what was real and what was fantasy? I had just left behind an intensely painful romantic relationship and no longer knew who I was. Clara came to me but not directly. I kept seeing the image of a beautiful statue in an enchanted garden. She was withdrawn from the sensual world. She was stone – white marble, similar to statuary or Carrara. She was alive, but she did not live. She could not smell the sweet, heady aroma of the roses surrounding her nor feel their red velvet petals brush against her stone hand in the afternoon breeze.

Clara inspired me to write this story. My mission was clear before I was born: I had agreed to write this book.

Most books are published into an ocean of indifference.

While there is a delicious freedom in writing a book as though no one may ever read it, Clara reminds me, this book is not for me alone.

So be it.

57

SADNESS

~ Memoir ~ Clara ~

Clara speaks to the Author:

Angela, this is the writing faith.

Sit in stillness and you will hear the words flowing through your heart. Take those actions inspired by your heart's desires – like those dance classes. Feel your energy soar. Your physical and energy bodies are in a rapid healing process. The experience is not always comfortable.

On occasion, spending the day in pyjamas will bring rest to your hyperactive mind. Your body needs breathing space before we begin the next phase of writing.

Thank you for your trust and open-heartedness.

58

INTEGRATING

~ Memoir ~ Author and Clara ~

Clara advises Author:

As your consciousness rises and expands, your perceptions will change. Allow time and space to integrate your new ways of thinking and being. Reflect on and accommodate your new desires. The actions needed will arise without effort. Some friendships will fade away while others will flourish. New people and resources will appear to meet your newfound needs as though on command.

Allow time to grieve the passing of the old ways but do not dwell in grief too long.

Be still within. You will sail through the stormy seas of your anger and anxiety. They are but a passing phase as you expel the demons that have tainted and shackled your spirit. You are not one to flinch easily. You will be fine.

Author replies:

How long is this phase going to last? It's so uncomfortable to be like this. Please not six months. Six days is bearable. Six months will be suicidal. I don't know if I can sit here any longer this evening. It's painful to write with no direction nor meaning to the words except the mutterings of dying demons. This disconnected feeling is hard to bear. Living in a world of fear and mistrust is horrible. I know that world is my creation – the chaos of my interior world at the moment.

The outside world has not materially changed. After a day at work, I still wait for the bus home in the cold night air, but my relationship with the outside world has changed. What was once the peaceful and serene order of things becomes an adversarial world seething with well-contained anger. At least I am aware of this rising anger. I do not know what it is about. A symptom of rapid healing, no doubt you would say. Is this the anger of awakening? I have tolerated mediocre circumstances in my life. I have had enough.

The next day my laughter returned in a spontaneous chat with my father. All is well. The gift in this experience has been to observe the chaos within me and remain still. It was a gift to see the external world as a reflection of my inner world.

Early that morning, Wednesday, 12 December 2007, I dreamt of a gorgeous white horse. He was a young grey colt, a fine bred animal with a beautiful spirit. In the dream, I promised him that someone would raise and care for him well. Only now do I realise that someone was me. My heart melted with love on rising from my bed. Taking loving care of such a creature would be reason enough to live a long and healthy life.

There are many reasons to live: to give freely of one's gifts – to burn brightly.

Better to be ashes than dust.

59

ACCEPTANCE

~ Memoir ~ Clara

Clara speaking to Author:

'Peaceful acceptance is impossible until you surrender old belief structures. Your mind built these beliefs to defend and control its existence. It created a world where your life seemed predictable, certain, but replete with drudgery.'

'Clara, are you being cryptic again? What does "surrender old belief structures" mean? What does that look like?'

'Remember, when you were a little girl growing up in south London. Your parents would experience dark moods. You could feel the inner storm of their anger rising for no logical reason. After many instances of sensing these frightening feelings in your parents, you imprinted that the world could not be trusted. Whenever you and your sister played as children around the home and you slammed the kitchen door by mistake, your mother would become angry, withdrawn, and depressed. You did not realise then, that sound of the slamming door in all its harsh suddenness, reminded your mother's subconscious mind of the incessant bombardment of her home town in Italy in 1944. For weeks during that war she endured the sounds which meant danger, destruction, and death. She was then only a child herself.

'Whenever you travelled long distances by train or by air, your father would become tense. You could sense his distress. You did not know then that travelling far reminded him of the civil war in his country, India, when he was just a teenage boy. He and his family were refugees in their own country, having to sleep on a train station far from home. Relatives were murdered before they could flee.

'You once believed, for example, no one could be trusted. This belief was reinforced by your lack of self-trust. You could not make any sense of your parents' inner turmoil. Their reality was alien to you. You were only a child. You could not have possibly comprehended the scale of their trauma. Maybe you did and it frightened you into believing that you were not fit enough to function in this world.

'You once believed you only deserved rewards in life through punishing hard work. This belief was reinforced by your lack of self-love. Your parents could not show how deeply they loved you when they withdrew into their traumatic memories. You imprinted that you were not worth loving because of some imaginary flaw in your divine being.

'You retreated to your reason and intellect and lived from your head instead of your beautiful heart.

'A useful quote by the scientist and thinker, Albert Einstein:

'*"Not everything that can be counted counts and not everything that counts can be counted."*

'An overactive mind is usually cluttered and inefficient. However, in a deep healing process, temporary over-activity in the mind is expected as old anxieties and dysfunctions are released. Allow yourself space to breathe. Do not fear, the writing flow will soon resume. Take time to build new strength and capacity: the flow will be far more powerful than ever before.

'Sit in peace. Be at peace. You are strong. You are enough.'

60

THE LONELY HOURS

~ Memoir ~ Author ~

Alone at my desk, when there seem to be no voices in my heart, I feel lonely.

Being alone and loneliness are not the same experience. Being alone and feeling Clara's voice through my heart is a great blessing, more joyful than any earthly celebration. I wish with all my heart I could hear her beautiful voice with my ears. Christmas is only ten days away. Bringing Clara's words to life is my deepest Christmas wish for 2007.

'You are on course for your destiny. Do not be concerned. Sit in peace and watch as the words tumble from your fingertips onto the screen,' Clara whispered into my heart.

'I'm scared of sabotaging myself through even more subconscious doubts and fears.'

'You know that will not happen. No need to be alarmed in seeing those qualities in others. They need to experience and resolve those for themselves. You can appreciate them with compassion without suffering yourself. You may feel faint memories in yourself of similar traumas from your childhood but know that they are clearing now over the Christmas holidays. By the new year, you will be a new woman, ready to hear my voice with all your power and love flowing from your magnificent heart.'

61

Play

~ Clara ~

My persistent disempowering thoughts become my limiting beliefs. They form rigid mental structures, strangling all joy out of my heart.

If I am desperate for a specific outcome, it leads only to my unhappiness. The greatest curse may be to receive everything I desire, believing that would make me happy. Instead, I may become more miserable than ever.

True happiness comes from within. Always.

Peace comes with the acceptance of the way things are. Acceptance, of course, does not mean I abandon up my dreams; it means being able to see things as they are while feeling neither defeated nor jubilant. I am at peace regardless. This is a creative state of mind, an enlightened one too.

Creativity is only possible through play.

Play is pure exploration with neither intent in being right nor fear of being wrong. The pleasure and excitement arise from discovery for its own sake.

62

DESIRE

~ Memoir ~ Author

'Clara, how do you manage your desires?' I asked her because I was never honest with myself about my desires, my deepest wishes and dreams. I had cut them out of my heart. Denying my desires was less painful than failing to manifest them.

'I did nothing. I have faith that if a desire is unfulfilled, there may be a higher reason unknown to me at the time and for my greater benefit. I was clear what my desires were and why I wanted to manifest them. The universe takes care of how they manifest.'

'You could let them go so easily?' I said.

'Yes, I released them. Holding on to a desire then denying it creates shadows in the heart and much suffering to the soul.' Clara's words stirred something deep in my heart.

'Could suffering be like depression?' I said. 'If I at least acknowledge my deepest desires, they'll become clearer. I don't worry about how they'll manifest?'

'This is the writing faith.' she said, 'Stand firm with a soft and open heart. Worry will prevent the manifestation of your desires. Clear the thoughts from your troubled mind by writing them down as they appear. All the complaints, all the fears, and all the desires too. They will heal and clarify as you write.'

I trust Clara: write whatever comes and it will all fall into place later with editing. I am grateful for the brief ray of sunshine this afternoon after the rain. Need to keep writing as the flow stays warm. When I stop, my rational mind kicks into action and all the creativity seems to go out of the window. Write from a heart full of love. The story will soon come alive again.

Clara speaks of writing while in a kind of trance: a conscious state where intense focus brings a sense of wonder and peace. Words are welcomed as they come through me. I do not judge the flow of words nor condemn them out of fear. Have faith in the process. My current consciousness may not always understand. Sometimes the ideas are beyond my current spiritual "pay grade". I am supposed to feel the words in my heart and not use my rational mind to explain and analyse every phrase as my old self would prefer. The story is beyond my rational mind and may only advance through leaps of the imagination. If I listen to my heart I may discover shadowy beasts in the darkness. They are projections of my long-denied self-longing to be embraced. They only wish to be accepted and loved.

I left London, the city of my birth, to travel thousands of miles to the San Francisco Bay Area. I met artists, writers, film-makers, Motion Picture Academy Award (Oscar) winners, Pulitzer Prize nominees. I met people who took their art seriously yet they took themselves lightly. They had the confidence to play and fail. They were the most generous people I have ever met. My British accent meant I could not fit in immediately. When asked what I was doing in the Bay Area, I explained I was writing a novel, that the main character (Clara) moved from London to San Francisco, and that I followed her to find out why. Their faces brightened in recognition of an authentic creative journey. They treated me as a real writer and artist. I had found my spiritual home.

I rented a lovely room in a friend's house in Berkeley. On late nights walking home from the Berkeley transit station, I would encounter deer venturing out of the state park and wandering the quiet streets of the Berkeley hills. They would not get spooked when they saw me as long as I was calm and tranquil. They would stop and watch me. One night, I came across a stag in a side street off Cedar. He had huge antlers. He stood proud, tall, and intimidating. I stopped walking and looked back at him in wonder. Without overstaying his good graces, I continued my walk home. A sedate pace seemed wise.

London is where I discovered that Clara is real. I always knew that in my heart, but my rational mind thought to indulge me as a passing insanity. Now my mind is silenced. I would love to hear Clara's lovely voice. How I would love the gift of clairaudience. All in good time. Psychic gifts bestowed too soon may bring fear and psychosis. Stand firm with a soft and open heart, she says.

I can feel her enigmatic smile.

Clara can speak into the hearts of those whose hearts are open. No use having an open heart if it lacks strength. No use having strength without knowing when to be soft and when to be hard. That is wisdom: flexibility of mind and heart. Some days discipline is needed. Other days, compassion. Wisdom is knowing when, why, and how. Discipline is necessary when the ego is invading the realm of the heart. Fear-based thinking interferes with the creative power of the heart. Self-doubts are poison and I must remain firm.

Here in my bedroom in south London, I have an eagle feather, a magnificent specimen, on the mantelpiece. A gift from Clara, I now understand, in response to my heartfelt desire for a small token of Aurora's and Polaris' energy. A blessing from Aurora herself no less on your instruction. Only a true desire from the heart can mobilise energies in the universe in ways that seem impossible to the human mind. But remember, all is possible in the universe or divine mind.

The greyness has returned after yesterday's sunshine yet each day the palm tree in my bedroom unfolds its new leaf. A gift from my mother. There is a little shoot coming up. A future leaf, opening next year perhaps. I write under one of the magnificent outstretched leaves. Parts of me are growing, that are new, like becoming an author. Parts of me are dying, like the desire I once had for a stellar corporate career. Life is too precious to dwell on past mistakes and misguided dreams of my younger years. I did not know about Clara then. I did not realise the extent of my spiritual wealth, but I am grateful for my life so far. The many lessons learned and failed have brought me here. Eager to learn more and grow.

I've heard it said that God is closer than my breath. I now see the meaninglessness of my human drama – the worries and concerns that occupy my waking life – and embrace my true divine self. I would see the same in others because we are all one.

Why does it seem easier to write at a full moon? The emotions are stronger and closer to the surface of my consciousness. In an industrial society, where the predominant thinking is with the rational mind, the heart or intuitive mind takes second place. However, around the time of the full moon, the rational mind may be overwhelmed. A man is more likely to ask a woman out for a date. Human beings are not rational machines but emotional beings. If humans were completely rational beings then commercial advertising would be a waste of time and money. Few people buy an automobile solely for its practical purposes. They buy for the emotions and feelings attached to the vehicle's marque and model. These emotions and feelings are carefully created and exploited by auto manufacturers, marketing and advertising agencies.

63

TELL THE TRUTH

~ Memoir ~ Author

17:38 GMT, Thursday 28 February 2008: The secret of freedom from emotional pain is to tell myself the truth. How do I really feel? I have lived so long divorced from what my heart says that my heart seems locked away in a bank vault and I can't find the key. Feelings are not comfortable, but it is through the darkness of the repressed parts of me that I will know God. It will be liberating to embrace the once shameful parts of me.

I am happy. Whatever strange sensation I experience now in spiritual growth I understand is part of the unfolding process. I can witness my states of emotion like anger, resentment, and depression, with detachment. They come from me. I am not a victim of some outside circumstance nor some vile, capricious god. There is order in the seeming chaos of life. The darkness I had wilfully suppressed in me, until now, is the chaos.

12:09 GMT, Friday 29 February 2008: A cold grey day. Hungry for spring but seasons cannot be rushed just because they seem unpleasant. My neighbour's pear tree is bursting with promise, each branch and twig proud with pale-green nodules of new life dancing in the wind. Look for the new life within me. The winds of darkness may be howling within me but let them pass. They cannot drown out the voice of God for long. This is faith: the understanding that all is well and always has been.

14:03 GMT, Friday continued: Look for the sunshine within me for it is behind the grey veil of illusion. The light is within. Look for God within. Do not fear the darkness as it is only the veil of separation – the ultimate illusion that we are separate, individual, and alone.

17:20 GMT, Friday continued: Bleak sunset. Dusk soaked in rain. Trees turning into angry silhouettes once more against darkening heavy grey skies. There is nothing to say right now and nothing to do except witness the outer manifestation of my inner world.

64

A Comet

~ James ~

James glanced at the television screen on his office wall. He usually checked the narrative slant and spin of mainstream news programmes. Of course, the full story is never for public consumption. The true context is hidden in plain sight with all mainstream media outlets and social media platforms under full control. He listens on a low volume setting while seated at his desk examining a pair of recently acquired swords.

Never before had he ever seen such magnificent artefacts. The intricate carvings on the scabbards and the hilts entranced him: a rose, a constellation, and maybe a meteor, but he could not decipher the symbols. With a slow tenderness he withdrew one of the swords from its scabbard as though unveiling a beautiful woman. The blade revealed ancient symbols etched into the metal which felt like steel but it was a strange colour. The scabbards, hilts, and blades were all the same colour metal – the darkest thundercloud grey.

The hilts were familiar. He had seen them before in a different form. With one hand holding a sword, he clicked on a previously read email from his operative in San Francisco and opened the attached photographs. He looked at the images again: Eleanor seated beside an unusual marble statue in Golden Gate Park – an alluring feminine form attired in robes and symbols signifying majesty and power. James zoomed in on the hilts of the statue's swords.

His gaze was drawn back to the television screen as he held one of the swords with both hands. The news anchor's restrained smile had softened as she completed the segment with an unusual story. An approaching comet will pass the earth so close, it will be seen blazing in daylight in the northern hemisphere. A rare phenomenon not seen since The Great January Comet of 1910. Most comets are visible only at night. They are usually fragments of larger comets broken up by gravitational forces as they pass our sun or a large planet in another star system. The comet, designated C/2021 M1, has remained intact. The Asteroid Terrestrial-impact Last Alert System, or ATLAS, centre in Hawaii calculated that C/2021 M1 could have previously passed the earth twenty-five thousand years ago and may not be due to visit our solar system again for another twenty-five thousand years.

James re-read his Iranian broker's message regarding the legend in detail. When he was negotiating the swords' price and delivery, he had only skimmed that part of the message. At the time, he was amused by the mercenaries' inventiveness; he had laughed at the preposterous assumption that he could be swayed by quaint folklore no matter how colourful.

But James thought again. The legends seemed too particular for the combined intellects of a bunch of war dogs hungry for lucrative retirement. The comet speeds between its perihelion and perigee, between the comet's closest point to the sun and its closest point to planet earth respectively, taking just one day before moving away from earth and eventually leaving our solar system. The power of the swords will be transferable to the current bearer on the destruction of the true likeness of the ancient warrior-sovereign in that limited time window.

James checked the ATLAS website for the projected time and date the comet was expected. Within twelve hours. Local daylight time in San Francisco was seven hours behind Zulu time or coordinated universal time.

He made a phone call to a subordinate and ordered his official helicopter to be ready for departure to meet his government jet at the military base in Maryland. He made sure to pack his hunting rifle as well as the swords.

65

Golden Gate Park

Aurora and Polaris flew high above the park. It was time. The thousand statues were restless in the soft afternoon breeze. The eagles calmed the statues with a coded sky dance that quelled any pre-battle anxiety. From high above, the eagles saw Eleanor and Richard walking towards Clara. David joined them, too, running a little further behind them.

David brought warning.

They did not have much time. Little did they know, the comet had just passed perihelion, its closest point to the sun, and was on its way to perigee, its closest point to the earth.

Eleanor faced Clara. Richard stood by and kept watch with his back to Clara. David kept watch too. Eleanor recited from the depths of her heart a Sanskrit chant that honoured the goddess of redemption and protection, known as Tara:

Om Tare Tu Tare Ture Svaha
Oh Liberator, liberate us from the suffering.

Within a minute, a chorus of dark contralto, tenor, and baritone voices rose from across the park and joined Eleanor in chanting the same prayer. The voices came from the formation of statues. This could not be. Eleanor continued chanting, undeterred by yet another instance of questionable reality. She wiped a tear from her cheek as she heard Clara's voice in her heart:

'Eleanor, I love you. Richard, I love you. David, I love you.'

Eleanor continued her chant, emboldened by the soaring voices in the park, from wherever they came. The earth trembled, a mild earthquake typical at this time of year, but Michael watched nearby, extended his mighty aura and stabilised the ground.

David looked around the park into the distance. A familiar figure approached. He was not wearing his usual sombre grey suit but dark combat trousers and boots, a grey T-shirt, a black military vest, military sunglasses, and a black cap. James held in his hands Clara's swords, unsheathed. The scabbards were slung over his shoulder with his bolt action rifle. It was loaded. At fifty metres, David and Richard saw the swords, formerly dull grey, become bright and shining. The walnut-sized diamond in each hilt came alive, too, sparkling and dazzling, almost blinding James with their brilliance in the afternoon sunshine. The swords' splendour was a stark contrast with the black plasma-nitrided steel of the rifle's barrel.

James stared at the swords in his hands for an infinite second. His once firm jaw was now loose, mouth open, and eyes bright and wide behind his sunglasses. His body remained still until his face and body contorted in shock. He dropped the swords to the ground.

The hilts had become heated to the point of almost scorching his hands.

James's icy rage anaesthetised the searing pain in the palms of his hands. He slipped the rifle over his shoulder and flipped the safety catch over to fire. He took aim at Clara. James exhaled and squeezed the trigger. A hollow roar from the rifle's barrel reverberated through the trees. Richard had jumped in front of Clara. The bullet from the .30-06 round passed through his heart. David had already pulled Eleanor, still chanting the prayer, to the ground, out of harm's way. The trees shuddered.

Richard fell to his knees and collapsed to the ground by Clara's plinth. His face bore an eerie expression of profound peace.

Clara's form remained standing while the rousing chorus of voices continued from the throng of the thousand statues. The earth tremors subsided. James lifted and pulled back the rifle bolt, releasing the spent cartridge from the rifle's chamber. He raised his firearm to take aim again at Clara, but the angel commanded the swords to rise in tandem from the ground where James had dropped them. They swirled together as one rotating disk, slicing through the air, singing their unearthly song, towards the angel. They turned and flew back in an arc towards James. The swords separated mid-flight, at the apex of their trajectory. One sword pierced James in the chest. He was blinded by Clarity's violet diamond flashing in the sunshine. A violent fountain of blood rose within him. A split second later, the sword Brilliance sliced through his neck and flew on back to the angel. James's head rolled off his shoulders. The cap fell away. His metal-rimmed sunglasses cracked and bent askew as his capless head thudded and bumped to the ground.

The comet appeared in the sky. Its huge tail stretched far and wide. It was on its way out of our solar system.

Aurora swooped down from the sky. Her talons grasped James's scalp from the ground. She soared high above the thousand statues, followed by Polaris who had picked up the rifle by its sling.

The thousand statues below disintegrated, crumbling twenty at a time, row after row of pink granite dust clouds rising and statue fragments falling, fifty rows in all.

The eagles flew far out to sea, high above the Pacific, and released their respective cargos into the ocean. James's head fell to the bottom of the ocean, buffeted and swayed by the currents. By the time the head settled onto the ocean floor it was no longer cooling human flesh but cold white marble. His shocked expression was now frozen for an eternity.

The chorus back on land softened. The statues had crumbled. One collective breath had surged through the columns of stone beings, releasing them all. David and Eleanor, still lying face down near Clara, saw a gleaming figure standing in the near distance where James had been.

James's headless corpse had transformed into a figure wearing light armour that shone like a mirror and a gem-studded sword belt set with a large cabochon ruby worn below the navel. The ruby gave a parting red flash in the sunshine. The splendour of steel and gems dimmed. The figure succumbed to a creeping ashen patina that, within minutes, paled to white until there appeared a statue of pristine marble replete with every exquisite detail of Xoran's regal armour.

Richard's body lay serene across Clara's plinth. His blood stained her marble form. She sustained some damage from the bullet that had exited Richard's left shoulder blade.

The angel Michael appeared again behind Clara with wings outstretched. He emanated an energy so powerful that Clara's statue cracked. The plinth, followed by the rest of her form, crumbled in an attempt to embrace Richard at her feet. The marble statue of a majestic woman became an inert pile of chalk chippings and dust across Richard's body. The roses withered at Clara's plinth. The velvet petals, once a vibrant scarlet red, shrivelled to a lifeless brown.

The eagles flew north.

Michael breathed over the pile of chalk and raised Richard in his arms, enveloping the body in his voluminous angelic robes. All traces of Richard's blood disappeared. The angel summoned the swords and their scabbards just as he had done at Xoran's camp on that day Clara refused to remember. The swords flew back at once and they, too, disappeared into the angel's robes.

The angel faded away. The trees sighed in sadness and bid farewell to their heavenly friend.

David walked arm in arm with Eleanor towards the headless marble statue. He picked up the spent rifle cartridge by the statue's feet and gave it to Eleanor. The cartridge was still warm in her hands. Eleanor shook as adrenaline convulsed through her body.

The world now seemed bizarre.

Empty.

66

Hello

~ Clara ~

I am with you always. Do not be sad. All must come to pass. All earthly things are temporary no matter how long they seem to exist.

As for James, his spirit is now safely imprisoned in stone. His disappearance was a mere ripple in the daily affairs of government. His former associates, confused by his disappearance, and mistrustful of each other, retreated behind their official roles and duties at the Department of Defense: all documents were quietly destroyed, with legal and financial dealings suspended indefinitely. Any rumours were quashed by an air of studied indifference; any desire to ask questions was heavily outweighed by the fear of censure for speaking of matters beyond one's pay grade and security clearance. The government department demanded the strictest obedience. Inquisitive individuals with the intelligence to think independently had either been warned or terminated with extreme prejudice.

At his office in Washington, DC, James's safe contained documents authorising payments to shell corporations at offshore banking centres that would have initiated clandestine military operations and precipitated a global war. He was due to sign them when he returned from San Francisco after destroying me. My swords lured him to me, promising him untold wealth and power.

The authorities in San Francisco were baffled and embarrassed by the mysterious destruction of a major art exhibit in the thousand and one crumbled statues. They could find no explanation for the appearance in Golden Gate Park of a marble statue of a headless man in regal battle-dress from an unknown ancient civilisation. The statue was eventually sold at auction and later donated to a thriving church. That church in turn became decrepit and disused on the edge of the 101 freeway south of San Francisco in Santa Clara County.

There are no coincidences.

In Iran, the original statues of my thousand warriors, deemed impossible to insure for shipment, also crumbled with no clear cause. Thousands of others remained intact.

If James had succeeded in destroying my sacred marble form before I was ready to leave, my spirit would have been lost in the hellish realms of fear and doubt for another twenty-five thousand years until the return of the Comet of Aurelius. There would have been continued war and destruction for thousands of years in the future. The human spirit would have never survived.

67

ELEANOR AND DAVID

At The Walter Aston Hotel in New York, even the elevator doors opened with sedate tranquillity. David stepped out into the foyer of the Jade Salon, a spacious Art-Deco function room. His eyes scanned the four hundred guests attending the fundraiser. Where was his wife? He'd agreed to meet her here after his business meeting downtown.

She was probably near one of the green pillars on the north side of the salon but there were too many people in the way.

Then he saw her. An elegant figure, tall and regal in a midnight-blue gown. Time slowed down. The very sight of her commanded his heart to stop. Her sapphire necklace sparkled as she leaned in to a circle of fellow guests. She laughed at a witticism usually reserved for such gatherings.

He caught her attention at last. From across the salon she gave him a bright smile and with a delicate bow, excused herself from the circle of guests. She walked towards him, her gown, a fluid column of satin, swishing with every step. They met in the middle of the salon. Chandeliers twinkled above them: crystal shards of light caught every jewel, every sequin, every thread of silk that adorned the guests, but the sumptuous colours and jewels were no match for the light in her eyes that evening.

He had never before seen her eyes shine that way. They seemed to scintillate.

'You made it,' she said as David kissed her cheek. He was so tempted to kiss her full on the mouth, but that would have smeared her lipstick in a public place which required a little more decorum. He planned to smear her lipstick later when they were alone at their hotel. The light in her eyes was even stronger the closer he came to her. It was as though she held some eternal, magical secret.

'Let's get some champagne,' David said.

'Not for me, darling, thank you. But I'd love one of their zero-alcohol cocktails.'

'Is everything OK?' David said. Even though his wife did not drink much alcohol, it was unusual for her to refuse one glass of champagne.

'Yes, absolutely. Stomach's been a bit queasy lately, that's all.' She smiled at him as they walked arm in arm to the salon's bar.

A few months later...

David kissed Eleanor's swollen belly and rose from their bed to begin his day. He paused for a moment to watch his wife sleeping and wondered at the power of her dreams. Their daughter stirred within her mother's womb in response to her father's kiss.

David walked away from the bed to the bathroom. Eleanor would most likely sleep a little longer. He brushed his teeth, showered, and began his shaving routine. It seemed to have been a lifetime since they met at Grace Cathedral over two and a half years ago. He had been watching Eleanor under orders from his taskmaster for a few months prior to their meeting, but she enchanted him the moment he first saw her leave her apartment in Berkeley.

Eleanor stirred on their bed. From the bathroom, David could see her pushing the comforter off her body and stretching her long legs. How did he become the luckiest man in the world? Their lovemaking had a passion that seemed beyond any possible reality. Their bodies together held a magic far beyond his understanding. David gave up trying to find a reason or a logical cause and instead surrendered to the flow of energy between and through them.

'Good morning, sleepy head,' David said. Eleanor had swung her legs over the side of the bed, facing the bathroom. God, she was beautiful even without a scratch of makeup.

'Good morning, oh glorious husband,' Eleanor yawned and stretched. She struggled to smile. Was there a slight sardonic tone in her voice? David smirked at the minor contention between them: her energy was slow in the mornings while he was bright, breezy, and full of annoying energy. Conversely, his energy would slow down early in the evening while Eleanor was still reading or immersed in one of her spreadsheets. He soon learned that her obsessive, compulsive focus on intricate details relaxed her.

Eleanor drank a bottle of water. Her usual half-litre on waking.

'I'll get the coffee going. We've got croissants too.' She put the empty water bottle aside, pulled on a cotton robe and went downstairs to the kitchen.

As soon as he thought he knew his wife, she would reveal yet another facet of her character and dazzle him with her quiet brilliance.

Eleanor's ability to make and manage money impressed him. Budgets, income, and expenditures would be logged in spreadsheets of her own design on her laptop. Ten percent of after-tax income would be allocated automatically to a budget for donations to non-profit organisations that shared Eleanor's and David's passion for a world of prosperity and peace.

Eleanor was frugal by nature, but through David's influence, they agreed to allow ten percent of their income for expenditures that would bring them joy. Eventually, Eleanor and David would donate the majority of their wealth to non-profit foundations that help the world's poor and disenfranchised to create and sustain healthy livelihoods.

Their unborn daughter, Clara, would be well taken care of financially but would not be burdened with the pressures of superficial acquaintances who may masquerade as friends – the social parasites who seek out those with a net worth beyond mere affluence.

David pondered the life their daughter would have in the future. What kind of world would it be when she reached his age? He would give his life to protect her, without question. He would do the same for Eleanor.

It did take a few months to persuade Eleanor to marry him. Her reluctance was not because she did not love him, but because of her fears of the legal entanglements marriage brings according to the jurisdiction of the ceremony. However, with careful examination of the marital and divorce laws of the State of California and a fair and transparent pre-nuptial agreement, Eleanor relented, releasing the last barricade around her heart, and opening her womb to new life for the first time despite her mature age.

David did not realise how healing his presence was for Eleanor. He would never know that all her irrational fears and neuroses faded away when he kissed her for the first time. His touch would help her discharge any emotional discomfort and excess mental energy as though they were an electromagnetic imbalance in her body. For him, she would always be a regal woman of intelligence, beauty, and grace. The occasional glint of steel in her character would never fail to excite him.

After breakfast, David left the house. He loved the drive from their home in the Berkeley Hills to his office in San Rafael. The firm in which he is a partner prefers to meet in person once per week at the simple but bright office-base-hub to ensure each employee has the right balance of support and challenge aligned with the direction the firm is taking. The culture was typical of new successful Northern California startups: openness and accountability within a culture of trust. Here, it was expected to fail in any of the small projects if the firm was able to learn and re-invest the lessons learned in larger more capital-intense projects. Any failure due to negligence was, of course, not tolerated, but the important part of the firm's culture was the freedom to fail in projects that were purely exploratory.

His firm attracted the finest minds from Stanford and UC Berkeley who loved to work in collaboration with other brilliant, passionate souls for the benefit of the firm's clients. Self-serving glory hounds soon found it impossible to gain traction in their grasping careers and would move to hot-headed new firms near Los Angeles.

In the following weeks, David spent more time working from home; Eleanor needed rest during the day as her pregnancy progressed. They had recently written a book together, a work of fiction regarding the thousand and two statues of Golden Gate Park. A non-fiction account would have been too strange to sell. David wondered how or where the ideas came from. He did not know that in her dreams Eleanor would see her friend, the once stone Clara, now vibrant and alive, inspiring and helping Eleanor write the story. David did not question the provenance of the ideas for the book, but instead, he checked facts and story consistency with the great satisfaction of being a useful husband.

68

The First Blessing

Clara's voice resounded in Eleanor's heart.

Eleanor could not decipher what her friend was saying, though Clara's majestic voice and compassionate tone were unmistakeable. Eleanor was seated, as usual, on the curved marble bench by Clara's plinth. An eagle called above. The golden eagle's whistle and whoop had the pitch and resonance of Aurora's unique call. Eleanor looked up at the summer sky and smiled.

An eagle call from above pierced Eleanor's consciousness and awoke her from a deep sleep. It was only a dream. Eleanor had frequent dreams of Clara, especially since her pregnancy with her first child, a daughter also named Clara. Eleanor turned on her daybed on the terrace of her home overlooking San Francisco Bay. Her belly was quite big now. It was hard to get comfortable when she rested in the afternoon sunshine. She was pregnant again with her second child, a son, to be named William.

She missed her friend's beautiful spirit. It seemed to shine through the Italian marble. She missed their telepathic conversations and rich meditative silences. She missed Clara's golden eagles, Aurora and Polaris.

A cool afternoon breeze from the ocean stirred the aroma of velvet red roses. The pleasing and familiar fragrance soothed Eleanor's aching heart.

Baby Clara slept, undisturbed in a cot next to her mother's daybed. Red roses grew in the flowerbeds around the terrace perimeter. No one had planted them there. They appeared just before baby Clara was born a year earlier.

From above, an eagle called again. The sound seemed closer this time. David ran out from the kitchen to the terrace.

'Did you hear that?' Eleanor said. She rose from the daybed.

'An eagle? Here?' David looked upwards but saw nothing but blue sky and a thin contrail from a lonely airliner. He was doubtful but was wary for the safety of his wife and infant daughter.

A dark shadow, swift and sure, moved across the sun. The sunshine fluttered. A large shadow scurried across the warm stone tiles of the terrace.

A magnificent golden eagle ascended over the balustrade. With a whistling turbulence of her wings she hovered, then perched on the edge of the cot with the sleeping infant. A crooked feather fell into the cot from her left wing.

Eleanor and David remained still, enchanted by the singing vortex of air whipped around them. The infant awakened, chortled at the beautiful bird, and clutched the fallen feather in her tiny hands. The eagle gathered her mighty wings and ascended with a slow cadence, rocking the cot. She flew over the balustrade towards the ocean before turning back, circling higher, and flying north.

'Clara,' Eleanor said, breathless. She picked up her daughter and cradled the infant close to her heart. The eagle feather was still in baby Clara's hands. The feather caressed Eleanor's cheek. Eleanor could barely speak. She sobbed:

'Clara, is it you? It's you. Oh my God, it's you.'

Acknowledgements

My rigorous and wise editor, Dr Liz Monument. My proof reader, Julie Hoyle. However, any errors or failings in this book are mine alone.
Harry Bingham and all the wonderful writers and tutors at Jericho Writers who demystified the whole writing process. Andrew Wille and Kellie Jackson at Words Away. Their fiction masterclasses were transformational for me. Authors, Ellie Anstruther and Tor Udall for their kind inspiration and encouragement. Jacqui Lofthouse, my wise mentor at The Writing Coach. Jacqueline Owens, my writing accountability buddy.
My spiritual mentors and friends Dr Wesley B. Morris, Jayn Lee-Miller, Janis Kembel.
Friends who also made the writing process far less lonely: Peg & Bob Miller, Yvonne Burgess, Leonard Pitt, Susan Griffin, Lex Williford, Charles Nickila, Steven Randall Roberts, Duncan Chatwin, Richard J Curtis, Jack Berriault, Mark Broderick, Carol Bamesberger, A.M. Noel, Dr Suzette Lue Chee Lip, Dr Fiona Marsden, Elaine Churchill, Dr MaryAnne Shiozawa, Helen Oakwater, Geraldine Dearden, Chris-

tine Kennedy, Adrienne Celli, Daisy Foss, Angélique Peigné, Susan Whyte, Jennie Jones, Donna Evans, Norah Marshall, Jessica O'Toole, Ria Danielsson, Michele Kelly, Shakil Dawood, Rachelle Gaskell, Takako Nakasu, Ania Pieniazek, Taniya Hussein. Francesca Blackwood, thank you for the beautiful smoky quartz crystal you gave me. It sits on my desk and inspires me with its otherworldly translucence.

My brilliant cousins Rupa Datta and Dr Vivek Datta. Vivek is a psychiatrist and recommended books for background research on James's character.

Dr Brigitt Angst, Stuart Whitehall, and Paul Ebentheur for their wisdom and encouragement at the Global Information Network.

My thanks to Rachelle Gaskell for introducing me to Marcel Van Der Merwe and Carl Groenewald. I thank them both for their exquisite perfume expertise and scent advice for James/Xoran, and David/Xavier.

UK National Rifle Association. Derek Stimpson, from the British Sporting Rifle Club for advice on James's firearm. I had no idea a hunting rifle would be so heavy in my hands.

My yoga teachers Em Thomson and Harriet Alexander. Their tough classes in south London kept me sane.

The British Library, London. The library, University of California, Berkeley.

For inspiration: Royal Botanic Gardens, Kew; University of California Botanical Garden at Berkeley; Golden Gate Park, San Francisco; Grace Cathedral, San Francisco.

Madeline Miller and the international success of her book, *Circe*. I met Ms Miller at her book-signing event in London's Waterstones bookstore in 2019. I will never forget how she looked at, and recognised, me as a fellow writer.

I am supremely grateful for the patient support from my parents, Ashish and Giustina Dutta as well as my wise sister, Monica, and her fiancé, Simon. If only Ma had lived long enough to see this book published. She smiles from heaven instead.

And for showing me the way, Clara, my muse and guide from another dimension.

Printed in Great Britain
by Amazon